'A story of life beyond co
ANTONY SUTCH - THOU

THE
DIARY
OF A
DIVORCE

Never give up!

I am Divorcing You

ISOLDE

The Diary of a Divorce

First published in 2019 by

Panoma Press Ltd
48 St Vincent Drive, St Albans, Herts, AL1 5SJ, UK
info@panomapress.com
www.panomapress.com

Book layout by Neil Coe.

Printed on acid-free paper from managed forests.

ISBN 978-1-784521-66-0

The right of Isolde to be identified as the author of this work has been asserted in accordance with sections 77 and 78 of the Copyright, Designs and Patents Act 1988.

A CIP catalogue record for this book is available from the British Library.

All rights reserved. No part of this book may be reproduced in any material form (including photocopying or storing in any medium by electronic means and whether or not transiently or incidentally to some other use of this publication) without the written permission of the copyright holder except in accordance with the provisions of the Copyright, Designs and Patents Act 1988. Applications for the copyright holder's written permission to reproduce any part of this publication should be addressed to the publishers.

This book is available online and in bookstores.

Copyright 2019 Isolde

DEDICATION

O Best Beloved

FOREWORD

The Diary of a Divorce is a novel in diary form which grips the reader through every twist and turn of this harrowing account of a mother's escape from a miserable marriage, to the cautious hope of some happiness at last, as she leaves the courtroom for the last time.

The author writes through the eyes of the diarist's estranged daughter, who chances on her mother's diaries and reads for the first time of the sufferings her mother endured whilst trying to protect her child from the terrors and abuse of a bitter divorce. Cecily's searingly honest diary entries revive old resentments as the narrator remembers how she felt as the young child torn in both directions by her parents' enmity. As she reads on, she discovers how little she knew and understood her mother and what she was going through during the marriage break-up. The reader follows her as the diary reveals to her astonishment that her mother had a hidden love, passionate yet with little hope of fulfilment, which kept her going in her darkest hours but increasingly filled her with despair as to the prospect that Francis would finally summon the courage to give up his comfortable but unsatisfying life, in order to be with her properly.

The final pages leave the reader wondering what the future holds for Cecily and whether this tale of misery is all there is, or if it will at last lead to happiness. As the narrator puts down the last page of the diaries, we feel her new understanding of her loving, but often awkward, parent and her hope that she too may now be reconciled with Cecily.

This book is both a tale of tragedy and a passionate love story, but it also serves as a vivid guide to the pitfalls of the divorce process. It carries the reader through each step of the process, from heart in mouth announcement of the split, to the endless legal documents and hearings which accompany the dismantling of the marriage vows. It is required, but rewarding reading for anyone contemplating ending their marriage; a stark warning of the rows and trickery, the endless delays and the dangerous blandishments of lawyers, who all too often are more focused on their fees than what is really best for the protagonists and their young children, too often the real but blameless victims of the process.

An enduring image is the warning to remember that time spent seeking consolation on the latest outrageous act from the ex-partner is best seen as lighting and burning wads of fifty pound notes one by one.

The Diary of a Divorce is a cleverly crafted and compelling account of one of the most disturbing experiences of modern life, yet one which is almost never written about. Each episode brings a new and unexpected twist, and the crisp but beautifully written narrative makes it impossible to put down until you reach the conclusion. I commend it to you and look forward to the sequel.

Andrew Roberts: *Churchill: Walking with Destiny* (2018)

'We all know that Art is not truth.
Art is a lie that makes us realise the truth.'

Pablo Picasso

PROLOGUE

When my parents divorced there was a lot of standing around on doorsteps being passed from one parent to the other. I knew perfectly well how much each of them wanted me to show a preference, so I was careful not to give either of them any ammunition.

I have not seen Little Woman (which is what I called my mother when I was young; she is tall, and I thought it was funny – "Little Woman" or "LW" for short), for years. I got so fed up with all the scrapping and residual resentment towards my father that it was easier to cut her off completely than to maintain the relationship.

After school I went to paint in Spain and stayed there, which has made not keeping in touch quite easy. LW left England about the same time, which is pretty irresponsible; even if I do not choose to talk to my mother I am still her child and she should be available. Ridiculous. Apparently LW now says she is never coming back to London, which I think is also pretty irresponsible; even if I do not choose to talk to my mother I am still her child and she should be available. Ridiculous.

Apparently our old house is up for sale now, and I promised the lawyers that I would see if there is anything worth keeping. Women particularly seem to hate letting go of anything that once mattered; as though letting go of the past devalues what used to be important. Which is rubbish.

You have to leave your past behind you though. If you stuff yourself up with too much past you leave no room for pudding, which is how I like to think of the future: it is the sweetness to come once you have eaten your greens.

I had a lot of greens as a child.

As we approach our street I tell the taxi driver to stop outside the café where my mother used to get her coffee when I was little. I used to go with her if she had forgotten to get breakfast for me or make my school lunch or something. We went there a lot. She had no interest in cutting sandwiches or boiling eggs, which are what little children need. Amazing I ever got fed at all given my parents' casual attitude to feeding me. Dad got a cook but that did not work because I was used to the feast or famine of LW's kitchen, and the starchy consistency of cook's regular meals made them indigestible. I felt disloyal eating another woman's food. Children can be complicated.

I order a cappuccino because it does not seem right going back to our house without getting a coffee here first. LW loved her cappuccinos even before they became the mainstay of the High Street economy. It is raining when I leave the café and the sky is grey and unforgiving. How to paint in England? Shades of grey presumably.

Smudgy childhood memories subliminally floating around the edges of my soul have necessitated my return. I need to nail a few uncertainties more definitively onto the canvas of my mind. There are things I never understood and smudges distort the picture if you are not swift with the white spirit. I sigh and a schoolgirl looks back, whether hoping to share my levity or glimpse a madwoman I neither know nor care as I have arrived.

I never had my own key so this opening of the door elicits no Proustian sequence. I went to boarding school before I was old enough to have a key and later when I came home, in sullen humour (some alternative arrangement must have fallen through for me to have returned at all), my mother would be there, bursting through the door all smiles and need, before I even had time to rearrange my face into the resentful look that showed her the suffering her uprooting us had caused.

The door was still the same creamy yellow she and I had (chivvied by my mother's indefatigable enthusiasm) painted it one summer. A bit chipped but still glossy as though shining hopefully out.

I smile at the memory of LW's delight when the strident, unforgiving red of the old door gave way to the creamy yellow. She really believed that a colour change could transform and soften the world beyond it. As though a front door could somehow shield us from any danger, if only we could just get the right hue. Is that why I paint?

I was unexpectedly overwhelmed by the pervasive pomegranate and amber smell of my childhood and went straight up to my mother's room as I had cleared mine out when I went to boarding school. I was not going to leave anything for Mama to investigate in my absence. LW was keen on nosing about into other people's feelings. She thought she was good at it too. I was so sick of feelings, I had pretty much decided not to have them any more.

I stand at the bottom of the stairs feeling unexpectedly peaceful until I see the wallpaper I had torn, demented by parental brainwashing or general misery. We never fixed it, I do not know why. You leave something long enough, the damage is absorbed into the general landscape, a rip in the wall on the ground floor. She did not get angry; worse. She came flying out of the kitchen, saw the tear in her pretty paper and just stopped and looked so sad that I spat venom. What right had *she* to look sad? I was the one suffering. I was the one who was hurt. All she cared about was her bloody wallpaper. I was driven into a frenzy of fury by that look of mourning, and something else I could not read but did not like. I raged on. I wanted her to rage back, not look so bloody sad.

I turn away from the broken bannister (more rampaging) as I trudge up the stairs, made bright and wide by her choice of paper whose flowers created light and space between them. She had tried to make it nice. I can see now that she had tried.

What lies behind the sage green door of what I had come to think of as her private apartments? Not too much I hoped but could not be sure because by the time she had decamped upstairs I was already too old to come knocking at her door for stories or cuddles. Or anyway, I was too old and far gone to admit to any needs. I was an angry girl, but I was a child and not to blame.

Was I, *am* I, still too harsh?

* * *

I had determined to bring my father's spirit into the house, to make Mama feel his forceful presence, the one she was so keen to keep on the steps outside. But I was still little then so had it been my will, or did I simply feel obliged to make her suffer as we did. All things being equal, as children like them to be on the whole.

* * *

I turned the handle of her bedroom door and held onto my heart.

God, she had left everything. She must have closed the door and stepped into another life. The cupboards and drawers were brim full of her stockings and endless 'cobwebby' dresses, as I used to describe her long chiffon numbers. I open all the drawers and cupboards and stand in this elegant room with silk and lace pouring forth, as though begging to be worn and admired again. Poor Mama, why had she left it all? I was not around when she abandoned England. Had she left everything because her exquisite clothes from this era were imbued with a fragility, which she wanted to discard?

I felt a sense of my mother's despair and continued gazing at all her finery, feeling my mother's presence with an overwhelming sensation of stepping back in time. I suddenly felt very lonely and weary, so I rolled over and curled up onto my side, closing my eyes and inhaling the heady scent of my childhood. I fall asleep. It is dark when I wake.

I found the papers in a fairly chaotic pile stacked on her desk, it was almost as though she had deliberately left them out for me to read.

There were some beautiful leather volumes, soft with age and crammed with notes but thereafter she seemed to have used whatever came to hand: napkin jottings between loose pages and I imagined her scribbling between coffees after dropping me off at school.

I used to ask her why she did not get a job if she was so worried about money and she would do that infuriating thing of saying: "I'm far too busy having pedicures, darling" because I had once told her that me and dad had spotted her having her nails done. Dad had commented that she should not spend her money on manicures. She went berserk, banging on about *deserving* hairy legs.

Later that day we were in Peter Jones and I asked her if I could have a new doll. She picked out a truly wonderful one with abundant flowing flaxen hair, a princess doll, and presented it to me. "Now this *is* how I should spend my money, isn't it, darling?" She beamed delightedly and winked.

I think I did at least have the grace to feel sheepish, even if I did not show it.

I gathered some of the books together and walked over to her comfy flowery armchair by the window and a single sheet fluttered to the ground.

It seemed to be some sort of cautionary note:

Remember Cecily, children have no malice, their cruelty is only a symptom of the unhappiness they endure and seek to source.

And there you have her: LW, Mama, my mother. Making everyone else feel guilty.

I read on.

As the battle waged on, I found I needed to record the odd anecdote about my divorce between the interminable court appearances and endless conferences with lawyers, because it is a lonely business and writing it down helped.

A bit.

I did not know I was going to fall in love along the way, so I wrote about that too, which helped.

A lot.

I was lucky. I found the love of my life. I thought I was lucky but somewhere along the line I seem to have misplaced a child. You never give up hope of finding the ones who wander off and cannot find their way back. You can give up on romantic love if it gets too tricky, but you never give up on your children.

* * *

If you are divorced, you think that whatever bad happens would not have happened if you had not left 'the father' as both lawyers and judges infuriatingly insisted on calling the man that I had finally summoned the courage to leave. My lost girl has always been good at impressing this upon me. If I had not left, everything would have been all right. Or, at least, much better.

My lost girl thinks I should have stuck it out and negated myself for her sake.

When she was three, she found me on the stairs, "Why are you crying, Mummy?" she asked as we sat side by side like Pooh and Piglet.

"Are you feeling blue?" she ventured, not meeting my eye.

How she knew about being blue I never knew.

Time to leave before the blue becomes the only hue, I think, gathering up the leather volumes and piles of paper and hastening down the stairs.

CONTENTS

Dedication	3
Foreword	4
Prologue	7
Chapter One	19
Chapter Two	23
Chapter Three	35
Chapter Four	39
Games	39
Chapter Five	41
Chapter Six	53
More Games	53
Chapter Seven	71
Chapter Eight	73
Chapter Nine	85
Chapter Ten	89
Chapter Eleven	91
Francis	91
Chapter Twelve	99
Chapter Thirteen	103

Chapter Fourteen	107
Chapter Fifteen	109
Francis	113
Chapter Sixteen	115
Chapter Seventeen	119
Court	119
Francis	127
Chapter Eighteen	141
Chapter Nineteen	143
High Court	143
Chapter Twenty	147
Chapter Twenty-One	153
Chapter Twenty-Two	157
The Mistress	157
High Court	159
Humour	160
The Settlement	162
Postscript	164
About the Author	166

CHAPTER ONE

"The Grizzly Bear is huge and wild;
He has devoured the infant child.
The infant child is not aware
It has been eaten by the bear."

AE Housman, *Infant, Innocence*

The Christmas before I left Gargoyle, I was lying one night with bruised ribs after our worst physical fight when the telephone rang. I managed to tell the caller that G was free that evening. G did go to the drinks and none of the locals were any the wiser.

I closed my eyes; I felt as though I was abusively invading her raw thoughts despite her tacit permission (she had after all left the papers out, so she must have known they were there and that I was coming). I felt a sense of trepidation. She is my mother and there are bound to be secrets she is now entrusting to me that I might not want to know.

I visualised LW: a tall thin blonde with untidy hair, using her long fingers as she waves elegant hands to weave a fantastical tale.

She looks helpless, a delicate creature tied down by her mannish shoes.

I recall white silk shirts of various hues, and a Coco Chanel dictum that women of a certain age should wear white near their faces because it flatters the complexion. She pairs her pale shirts with skirts, in fine linen or worsted silk… impossibly impractical. Ridiculous.

Her sad green eyes look up at me through long, pale lashes. Her face is translucent.

She has a wide mouth prone to laughter, and gets freckles easily, so she used to wear glorious wide brimmed hats in the sun.

LW, Cecily, my mother.

* * *

Remembering all this transports me back to my seven-year-old self and makes me sad; whether for her or me, I do not know. I cannot picture her differently from the way I remember her, so there she stays – aspic Mummy. I have not seen her since she left England. She has never offered to come to the gallery in Madrid or even to visit me in Spain at all. She has never even seen any of my work. My parents are both still alive and probably still kicking each other for all I know. Sometimes you just have to look back in anger and move on. She could have come to my first exhibition, but it seems she just lost interest and moved on – despite what she says about how hard it is to abandon

CHAPTER ONE

your child.

I am curious about her love affair. Odd she never mentioned it to me, another secret.

* * *

If you have children, protecting their hearts and minds should dissuade you from expressing anger toward your spouse, no matter how justifiable it may feel.

Well she failed there. She was always angry, even when she did not show it, I could sense it seething beneath the surface, only waiting for a supporter to call so she could erupt into a stream of vitriol against my father. Just because she did not actually say any of it to my face did not mean I was any less aware of it.

I remember Elizabeth commenting that I looked as though I was in a trance on my wedding day. After the deed was done, we did not consummate it; for two days I remained in a catatonic state, lurking fearfully in the old cave behind my mind. I was waiting, waiting to wake up and feel I was rooted in some way to my new surrounds. Eventually I learned to pull on the role of wife and mother rather as you pull on a pair of Marigolds. A girl in rubber gloves looks convincing and efficient even if she hasn't a clue where the washing-up liquid lives.

I learned to swallow loneliness down into dark pockets about my person that spewed forth their contents in the hell hours that insomniacs dread (usually between 3am to 6am, before the sun comes up, and the untangling can begin) but there are pills, as my new husband quickly discovered, to manage these things. He would feed them to me if I got troublesome. He was always terribly efficient with the pills as it gave him a role – and control – and perhaps he meant well.

Bloody hell.

CHAPTER TWO

"Mitte sectari, rosa quo locorum

Sera moretur."

"Stop looking for the place where a late rose

May yet linger."

Horace, Odes book 1, no 38, 13

James, once my boyfriend and now my dearest friend (why, oh why didn't I marry him instead of Gargoyle?), tells me I should get a lawyer now – even before I actually leave – Gargoyle's just worked out what he thinks it will cost to feed both me and our child if I now shop at Asda instead of Waitrose.

G looks up from his discount feeding frenzy and glares at me, "I cannot think of any expenses other than food can you?"

G had inherited his money (of which there was, it seems, a lot) and spent his time counting it, down to the last penny, and calculating the interest it was accruing in the well-concealed accounts where he secreted it. I have not a clue about housekeeping as he controls the finances and gives me 'pocket money' for sundries (coffees and taxis) and a Peter Jones card for groceries and household items. No money for new clothes, but I was not very interested in my appearance by then so that was not important. I bought my face creams at Boots.

* * *

"Car insurance? Council tax?" my lawyer later queries gently.

G's got millions so money is not going to be an issue, surely.

Or so I thought...

* * *

G goes on to ask about the dog, which he is welcome to, and in the same breath he suggests, "I will take Colette in the week, and you can have every other weekend and half the holidays. It is a simple and cost-effective solution, solving any issue about access arrangements."

I assumed he was joking but James gets quite heated about securing me legal representation when I recount G's solution.

Typical exaggeration. Of course he was joking.

* * *

I did not think the Gargoyle would mind if I left. He did not seem very interested in me nor indeed in Colette before but is now behaving strangely, locking rooms against me and I cannot even get into the wine cellar now, as I discovered when he was away for a few days.

CHAPTER TWO

I need a lawyer because I have received a letter from Gargoyle's new solicitor, which I find impenetrable. I do not ask my friends because, to other people, divorce is as boring as photos of your children.

I get up from the stairs where I have been sitting reading the first volume, my arms full of her books and papers, and I venture into the kitchen for the first time, more flowery wallpaper - it was everywhere, a triumph of hope over reality (the house has no garden but feels like a bloody park). I found the kettle and made myself a cup of tea — weirdly, even the food shelves are still stocked as though LW has just popped out for a moment. I carry my drink and 'revelations' to the kitchen sofa and, braced with sweet tea and with bated breath, I read on.

James arrives with a list of lawyers for me to choose from. Raymond Tooth services 'the disgruntled wives of rich men' according to Legal 500 (the legal bible, apparently) and is a bulldog where financial settlements are concerned. I do not want to use him though, because I do not want to be inflammatory. Gargoyle always says he has spent his life investing his inheritance to enable us to live in luxury, so I am confident he will provide.

James looks dubious when I explain this (he has met G) but accedes to my optimistic (naïve) assessment. I am, after all, the one who has been married to G for 12 years.

Latterly, my chosen lawyer emits a cough when I reiterate my financial confidence in G's inevitable financial generosity and lowers his gaze to the documents in front of him.

* * *

Later in the week when I am clearing out the general rubbish amassed during our marriage, I find a love letter I had never sent. There had been nowhere for it to go.

* * *

After my 'find a lawyer' lunch, James walks me to the tube and I exclaim, "I have just realised that I might be on my own for ever now. I will probably never be with anyone again. A life unshared. I never wanted to be divorced."

James says nothing and I prattle on.

Silence.

"I did not want this for my child. I wanted to protect her from the gory childhood I endured."

James resists retorting, "Well if you had married me you would not be in this predicament."

But he has never alluded to our past since the day I screwed my courage to the sticking post and told him I was going to marry someone else. That is how James is.

I have absolutely no idea what he thinks about any of it, or even if he thinks about it at all.

We walk towards Chancery Lane in the sunshine. "If I stay, Colette will assume marriage is sad and make bad choices for herself."

Like I did.

CHAPTER TWO

You stay for the children, and you go for the children.

James makes sincerely reassuring noises.

Why *did* I leave James? He was lovely.

I have not a clue.

"You are in a perfect position," he continues.

What can be perfect about any of this, I wonder?

"You have got Colette, and you are still fragrant and lovely."

And there it is, a fleeting allusion to our past: the 'fragrant' phrase being a reference to the judge's famously ridiculous description of Mary Archer, whose 'fragrant loveliness' effectively got her husband off the hook. This silly phrase had become a kind of shorthand between us for the madness of the judiciary system (James is a lawyer).

I feel an unexpected lightness of being as James warms to his theme.

"And independently wealthy. You are the ultimate catch my dear."

I am encouraged because in one fell swoop James has managed to make this Sordid Matter, into a Positive Thing.

Such kindness in him, I had forgotten.

"I had not imagined life *after* G," I reply, and feel quite perky at the thought. What if... a prince at last!

* * *

Later I remember how, as a child, I learned to catch the glint of excitement in the grownup's eyes, (I had to tell someone what was going on, and my parents were too consumed by the carrion of their own wormy passion to be available to the outpourings of misery from their own offspring), as my various confidantes and 'well wishers' subjected me to quizzing about the latest domestic occurrence at home. I soon learned how to spark their interest and so gain for myself the adult attention I craved,

"And then the police had to be called…"

I would say as I recounted in lurid detail the latest episode in what was a thrilling drama, unless of course it happened to be your life.

My parents had a disintegrating hold on the convention of, *pas devant les enfants*. And anyway, you do not need to be a linguist to recognise deranged behaviour.

LW never mentioned her parents, and Dad had told me they were dead. Strangely, after LW left, Dad invited them for Christmas – and they came like a shot, which I found weird. It made me feel disloyal to LW, and I did not like them one little bit.

* * *

Any concern I might have harboured about falling in love with my matrimonial lawyer evaporates as the lift disgorges Mr Puffle when I first visit Untying, Knot and Partners.

CHAPTER TWO

I wonder if one so ugly might make a formidable adversary. When he looks up at me, I notice his moustaches and struggle to contain my mirth. O joy! My very own Petit Poirot!

I had forgotten how searing my mother could be when she meant to be funny. There was never any malice intended. In the same vein, she had called Dad "the Gargoyle" since he had shown a proclivity for erecting monstrosities on the roof to provoke planning officers into raging battles. I suppose he got bored having nothing to do. Probably why I paint, battle with the elements, people are a pain in the ass.

* * *

Mr P ushers me into the lift with unctuous civility, and his odour overwhelms as the doors close.

We sit and he asks me questions I cannot answer; I do not know what G's net worth is or if my name is on the house deeds.

Mr P forgives my ignorance and is *delighted* to represent me. I am the perfect catch it seems, wide-eyed and innocent.

I am pretty sure that this is not what James meant. No empathy, just fees.

Matrimonial law is a commercial enterprise not a social service. Naïve women are excellent fodder for matrimonial lawyers, whose business it is to rack up as many billing hours as possible. Vulnerable women make excellent clients in this regard.

He would have represented G if he had asked first.

"Roughly how much is your husband worth?" Puff queries, and I am tempted to spit, "Nothing!" But he means money, and I do not know about that.

I have not a clue as it transpires, and my carelessness counts against me. Puff says if I had been more demanding during the marriage, my 'needs' in terms of the financial settlement would have been judged far greater, if you leave a (rich) husband the judges make allowances for frivolous expenditure when calculating your 'needs' post-separation.

Should have had more manicures after all.

* * *

I feel very light-headed as I leave Untying, Knot and Partners.

The petition will be sent to the home we still share and horror will ensue. Hitherto I have done as I was told by G during our marriage, and he is fierce when crossed. I tell no one that I am leaving him. I am sick with fear but long for the post to arrive and for the worst to be over.

* * *

I am leaving him. I have to go through with it because I am drowning. Poor Colette how will she cope? My GP said not to worry because children are happy if Mummy is happy, and she does not see Daddy much anyway.

Well, I would have seen him a lot more if she had not carted me off, but 'hands-off' fathers do not count, apparently.

CHAPTER TWO

Petition arrives. Horror. Gargoyle locks me in the kitchen and bellows,

"You do not know what you have done!"

I have made a dash for freedom before I become a prisoner of my own fear and drown in solitude and misery.

He rants and rages and I cower in corners.

The lawyers have demanded he put my name on the deeds of the house (as is my legal right) and he is *outraged* at having to do as he is told.

No mention of Colette or sorrow at losing us, just fury over finances.

I feel disembodied, but the first blow, surely the worst, has been dealt. The rest will be administrative. When do I go, and what do I take, apart from Colette, obviously?

My position is easier than for people who do not have a second home to go to. At least I have somewhere to live.

* * *

A few days later, Gargoyle proudly presents me with the telephone number of the Marriage Guidance clinic I begged him to come to last year and tells me to make an appointment immediately.

His solicitor has told him that courts frown upon couples who do not mediate. Gargoyle wants me to be seen to have refused to resolve things amicably. The first of many twisted tactics.

* * *

Puffle does not believe I do not have a lover, because even my family have sided with Rich G.

"How do you survive?" Puff enquires unhelpfully.

* * *

G takes Colette and the nanny away for a few days and a neighbour telephones while I am packing. She insists I go and have supper with them before my departure that evening. The notion of taking much besides bedding and books seems unnecessary as I still assume that the settlement will be ample.

Had I known how long and hard the legal battle would be, I might have been more grasping, but elegant coffee cups seem a small price to pay for 'A Room of One's Own'. So I take the absolute minimum, which is a mistake... possession really is nine-tenths of the law.

I am pathetically grateful for the neighbour's offer of supper (it is a dreary job clearing out a marriage). I had assumed any 'joint' friends would all be as keen as my family to stay in with the Rich Husband, which is why I had not bothered to tell anyone about my imminent departure.

I come in from the garden – I cannot bring myself to let my plants go to seed – to a message saying my neighbour's family has come down with 'a mystery virus.'

Supper cancelled.

I assume this woman was instructed by her husband 'not to get involved'.

CHAPTER TWO

The husband of 'she with a mystery virus' is a decorated soldier, but few people stick their neck out for something that will go publicly unrecognised.

In the scheme of things, the cancelled evening was no more than a distressing hiccup.

It was very distressing.

Reg	Forename
3Aspen	Aaryan
3Aspen	Abigail
3Aspen	Avi
3Aspen	Caitlyn
3Aspen	Deniz
3Aspen	Dorota
3Aspen	Eda
3Aspen	Ela
3Aspen	Eric
3Aspen	Freddie
3Aspen	Havin
3Aspen	Ismail
3Aspen	Janell
3Aspen	Joel
3Aspen	Julia
3Aspen	Kaya
3Aspen	Kinga
3Aspen	Kingston
3Aspen	Leon
3Aspen	Luca
3Aspen	Mariami
3Aspen	Nayser
3Aspen	Nhamo
3Aspen	Nihat
3Aspen	Rama'Hno
3Aspen	Romeu
3Aspen	Tayveon
3Aspen	Tyron
3Aspen	Xchyler

CHAPTER THREE

"Nam tue res agitur, paries cum proximus ardet."

"For it is your business, when the wall next door catches fire."

Horace, *Epistles book 1, no 18, 1 84*

Meanwhile, G treats me like an unwanted stranger. If I move to sit in a chair, he is there first.

The lawyers say 'Domestic Services' must cease, and I must throw the remains of my supper away lest he eats them!

I concentrate on my marrows, chopping, peeling, and cooking them before carefully placing them in the freezer (which I will never return to). I had planted and nurtured them though, and I cannot just leave them to rot.

Ridiculous.

It was all I could do.

* * *

I telephone Randolph as I set off to London. I need someone, somewhere to know where I am. He reassures me, "Just drive slowly and call me when you arrive so I know you are safe."

I feel floating, disembodied and Randolph's voice grounds me.

The traffic is at a standstill for ages and when at last it begins to creep forward, I can no longer tell if it is us moving or the oncoming traffic moving past us.

I make it to Heston Services and crawl off the road. I stagger into the Travelodge and ask the man at the desk to phone a taxi company for two drivers, one to drive me and the other to follow in their cab to take both of them back when they have dropped me off.

How did I manage to make this eccentric request understood? (With ease, as you do in extremis) and then I go to McDonald's and I pour lots of white sugar into stewed brown tea because the 'just in case something happens to my child' scenario is never far from a mother's mind, and I must stay alert, if only for Colette's sake.

I return to the Travelodge where two beaming Indians are waiting to help me get myself and the car home. We arrive at the house where they courteously enquire whether I need any further assistance before disappearing back into Wonderland from whence they seemingly came.

I do not often strike gold but this was seamless.

CHAPTER THREE

I remember the tale of her two drivers. She made it funny. It sounds quite surreal. Randolph sounds nice. She has always had good friends.

* * *

Tracy is very entertaining about bumping into the Gargoyle on holiday with Colette later that week,

"Cecily's not here." He announces.

"She has gone off holidays." He snaps at Tracy who is rooted to the spot, riveted by his revelations.

"She has gone off abroad completely."

He pauses,

"In fact, she has completely gone off me too!"

"That is a lot of information for 10 o'clock in the morning!" Tracy muttered as she beat a retreat and called me for the lowdown. "I did not know you had left," she squealed.

'Virus family' is keeping mum, it seems.

Tracy. Another 'friend' I never hear from again.

* * *

Orson says it is funny when I recount anecdotes about G. I can be funny about it, but God help anyone who laughs before me. Same principle as being rude about other peoples' families. They can say what they want but beware of joining in lest you overstep the mark by crossing some mysterious boundary.

* * *

Staying friends with both parties rarely works. It is infuriating when your friends see your ex-partner when you are in the throes of divorce. Why are they always so keen to *tell* you about him?

Why is he contacting my girlfriends anyway?

CHAPTER FOUR

Games

"For when the One Great Scorer comes

To mark against your name

He writes – not that you won or lost

But HOW you played the Game."

Grantland Rice, *Alumnus Football*

But it does, doesn't it and in this process very few do (play the game, that is).

Gargoyle fails to complete his Form E (sworn financial declaration of your net worth). Rich people are notoriously slow, too busy working out what they can squirrel offshore presumably. Why doesn't Gargoyle settle the finances so we can present a calm front, surely the key to a child's stability?

Maybe he hoped if he made it financially tricky, she might go back? He'd lost his family for God's sake, it is not surprising he was irrational.

I find myself worrying Colette will not be asked on play-dates when I am divorced because women think you might catch their men if you are single and men think that divorce is contagious.

Goodness, it is lonely out here.

CHAPTER FIVE

"And I was filled with such delight

As prisoned birds must find in freedom"

Siegfried Sassoon, *Everyone Sang (1919)*

Pat Barker's book *Regeneration* reminds me that I am divorcing, not foreseeing my death or waving a child off to the trenches.

* * *

I met Francis when I was married and it was a *coup de foudre*... but we were both married.

It seems I know nothing about her at all! Had my parents always been so unhappy together? Did she leave because of this bloke? If she had affairs, why was she so lonely?

That eventful meeting was at a local dinner party I had gone to with my then husband. The usual suspects (new faces are thin on the ground in the rural enclaves of well-heeled suburbanites) all stood around in a cold drawing room – some genius having removed all the radiators ('frightfully bad for the furniture') so that the guests all had to hover around blowing cold air at each other, presumably consoled by the beauty of their host's antiques.

With the familiar atrophy of heart at the prospect of the evening before me, I stood there, champagne in hand, wondering how not to drop a stitch from the dreary, little tapestry into which my life was so tightly woven, all hope of any joy beyond the sweetness of children, already ashes by then.

I shivered and glanced hopefully, or rather desperately, into the fireplace of that bleak room. There were coals in the black grate emitting pitiful little puffs of smoke, a blocked chimney perhaps, or just no current of fresh air strong enough to draw them to life?

Mastering the art of repetitious discourse on how Little Johnny is enjoying Eton and what a marvelous day's hunting it was, had become my life's work. So, I threw back my head and tossed my champagne down in one inelegant slug to enable me to respond appropriately to these electrifying topics. I knew that without the booze my impatience was occasionally inclined to rear its ugly head and boredom veer unsteadily towards visible irritation. And that would not do at all.

At that moment my attention was caught by the late arrival of another couple and I watched mesmerised as they drifted apart almost immediately upon entering the room, almost as though driven by an imperceptible undercurrent. Waves greeted her and drew her deep into the sea of social motion and undulating sounds of delight and expostulations and there he stood for a moment, quite alone, as though held back by the very undertow which had propelled her into the crowd.

CHAPTER FIVE

I watched him fascinated by his outward stillness and inner vitality. As she embarked on her journey amongst all those jolly county vessels, he ventured a hooded look around the room and I watched his face register a myriad of responses to what he found about him.

I recognised his resignation to the evening of familiar boredom ahead of him. I saw him plotting from beginning to end almost the exact course the evening before him would take. I saw him recognise it, dread it, resign himself to it and lastly gather his strength to endure again with excellent good grace what he reminded himself he must, albeit bewilderingly, deserve. It was this half buried, childlike bewilderment at the circumstances he found himself in and the route his life had taken to bring him here that gripped me. The heart of the matter, and the man, were revealed to me in those few moments. He was a man of many masks, which came away before my gaze. The mask of urbane sophistication concealing a fragility unsuspected by any who thought they knew him. He was totally at ease in these surrounds and yet quite absent. And no one had ever noticed.

I saw the man he was and I fell in love with him.

* * *

What had taken him so long to come? I had to repress some inexplicable irritation at his tardy entrance into my life. Never mind, my proper destiny had arrived at last. What course it would take was obviously unknowable. I was perfectly level-headed, assuming years of unrequited longing now lay ahead of me. But any fear of disappointment was already consumed in the desire to hear him speak. I knew he would come and so I waited for him to loop around the crowded room and make his way straight to me, as though dragged by the same force that rendered me transfixed.

The conscious certainty of our destiny was all mine. For years I had nothing, but my faith and, what must have subsequently seemed to him, my almost unworldly patience.

It was like meeting the embodiment of the internal voice that had given me the courage to find a path through horror all my life. My invisible childhood friend had taken on a physical presence. Years were to pass before I saw him again, but I thought of him every single day.

We had only just met, but I knew, as you do. Sometimes you just do.

So that is how I survive – blind faith that one day the honey will be for me.

I sat on the edge of my seat at that party when we first met, straining not to miss a word he said. He was gentle, observant, and funny about things. He commented on everything around us with insight and unusual wisdom, which allowed him to acknowledge the frailties of his fellow men without seeming to find the frailties an obstruction to enjoying life as he found it.

Oh well, how does anyone explain the tension that can exist between a couple that drives them to be together on whatever level they can be, despite the sometimes tricky moral compromises that must be negotiated to get them there?

CHAPTER FIVE

The man, Francis, looked at me so intently as I was scrabbling to find the words that would tell him what I needed him to know, and quite unexpectedly he offered, "Someone should give you a big pot of honey."

And so the complicity was established. He could see I was very sad. And I felt hugely consoled, like the relief of a lost child who has despaired and then is found.

Perversely my heart lurched and felt dark at him not minding that someone other than him might provide the honey. It seems ridiculous, but I was horrified. He could see it all. How could he not see his was the only honey I would ever want now? That would be sweet enough for me.

He was not conventionally handsome but possessed a soft expressive face, which revealed all his thoughts as they flashed through his mind when he forgot to hide them. He was in his early fifties, like everyone else at the party (I had married an older man), and he used his hands expressively, like an Italian, making pictures in the air as he spoke to me. His alert eyes twinkled with a readiness to smile that made me want to tickle him into giggles. I sensed he did not get much opportunity to share his mirth; his grownup world being too stiff and conventional for the gentle self-mockery he seemed so inclined towards. He gently poked fun at pretty much everything on show that night, especially himself.

He was scintillating but with a humility and kindness that belied his steely mind.

The other men that evening were all dressed in black smoking jackets, de riguer at county do's, but Francis had worn too many uniforms in his life I think and eschewed the sombre black velvet for a ravishing midnight blue velvet with a wildly unexpected azure silk lining I spotted when he leant back to allow the waiter to fill his glass, (staffed parties in county hell, do not you know!) revealing a softness bordering on frivolity even, beneath his conventional attire. His shirt was of white silk, a little frayed around the collar, a favourite shirt then, and he was sure enough of his status to dispense with the ghastly bow tie so much in evidence that night. Even his pale blue socks looked silky. I had to restrain myself from brushing my hand against his jacket for the pleasure I knew the velvets and silks would afford.

Everything about him was understated and elegant and thrilling. I was enthralled.

Half way through the supper party my horrible husband demanded I drive him home.

I dutifully pushed back my chair, mumbled goodbye to the most scintillating person I had ever met and left.

Why would I lay myself out like a doormat?

I was a successful journalist and television presenter once; where did all my confidence go? How did I get so downtrodden so quickly? And everyone knows good looking people have the world at their feet.

Oh but the judging and the misjudging and you cannot tell anyone because no one believes and they sneer at you and your complaints, how could anyone with all your gifts and blessings be anything other than the ruler of all she sees?

CHAPTER FIVE

Francis had seen it all in a moment; he had espied my sadness and tried to comfort me, reassure me I was not unpleasant or limited in my inability to find any soul mates or anyone of any interest at all amongst these county hunters I was living amongst. He found nothing wrong with me for finding county life narrow and difficult to contend with and agreed that the county's rather privileged world of hunts and shoots and parties was no excuse for a life, rather a weekend escape from it,

"I work in London," he said, "I would go mad if I had to live in the country all the time."

It sounds absurd but I felt so relieved and liberated to hear him say this; as I was then living with a man constantly accusing me of being deficient and objectionable because I found the country life so lonely and boring. I did not like admitting the bored thing because that does sound lame, but now years later I hear other people explaining their return to town for just this reason and I find myself agreeing with them; bored, bored, bored and what is wrong with that?

Nothing!

So why couldn't I express it then and take action? I hate myself for my passive inability to defend myself – ever – and to express my needs at all. As though to admit you require anything other than what is offered is to show a shameful and disgusting greed for which you will be spanked and slapped, jeered at and humiliated. And then sent to bed with an empty tray in the end anyway.

I suffered from anorexia as a teenager, so there does

seem to be a pattern of self-effacement, which does not actually make my spinelessness any less weird, worse actually as the pattern shows a void where you might hope to find a gentle rise in the learning curve; I was still the same fool scraping her existence between the thin ice of coping and freezing despair.

And so we left. I drove my 'tired' bully home. Oh and my heart was aching, the physical pain of dragging myself away from such a source of honeyed happiness.

A spark of hope rekindled as I drove us home that night. All was not lost, I was just Aurora waiting for her prince to revive her with a kiss. A prince's kiss would give me the courage I need to climb out of the marital tomb.

I was elated the following day. I took so much courage from the idea that there was someone who did not find me repellent and incompetent, but engaging enough to be worthy of watchful commentary. A tiny spark shot through me making me tingle with excitement. I remember so well driving along with Gargoyle and feeling so happy that everything had opened up for me, and that life was suddenly full to bursting with possibilities, like a fat ripe peach waiting for me to take a great big mouthful of it. Life was suddenly inexplicably sweet. I can remember feeling the same sense of excitement when I was much, much younger and had met a boy I liked and hardly knew, but even so, the whole world was suddenly shining for me.

* * *

I knew I would see him again. There was no more rational plan than that; for now the thought of him was enough to lift me from numb existence to some possibility in the air, something faint but exciting, like a walk in the country and finding your senses unexpectedly assaulted by the pervasive scent of Jasmine that creeps up in that magical blue hour which descends imperceptibly as you dawdle along.

* * *

I stumble alone through my divorce hell, surviving on this chink of hope. It is something at least.

I *galloped* on through the text hoping she would return to him and reveal her secrets, but she disappears from view again, which is absolutely typical.

Conversation with Colette driving home from school today,

"Why do you not come to Lurch House any more Mummy?"

I take a deep breath. This is a big question and I know she will always remember what I say next. I have no idea what to say next so I slow down and think hard. I must try to make it light because she is little. I hear words coming out of my mouth and listen to see if they sound ok,

"Well daddy and I find it hard to be together without fighting."

"Well, why did you marry him then?"

Unanswerable.

Colette (petulant now), "I want to live all together again."

Tears.

My mouth goes dry. What do you say to ease a child's confusion and protect them from the terrifying instability that divorce causes?

"Yes, but I do not," I say and go on to list the advantages of our new life.

I hear Colette snivelling in the back seat and my heart swells up into my throat, my chest feels constricted.

"I want to go back home, Mama."

"I was very unhappy before, darling, and my friends are here", I tell her. This conversation is too painful. I want her to stop. I feel guilty but I had to take her away from the misery. I did it for Colette's sake as much as my own. Didn't I?

Colette, with the abrupt change of mood that children are so unexpectedly capable of, starts listing those of my friends she likes the most.

I push on, "Life is not just about you, my lovely. I know it is hard, but I was very unhappy. Life is about compromise after all."

I could see that from her point of view I was not compromising at all.

But she had moved on, "What are we having for tea? Can we stop and get a pastry, please? My lunch was squishy and yucky. I threw it in the bin."

CHAPTER FIVE

"Oh darling. Poor you, you must be starving?" I was watching her like a hawk in the rear-view mirror.

"I do not think tomato sandwiches are for school because by lunchtime they are disgusting!" she pulled such a funny face that I burst out laughing and then we giggled together and were ok again and the relief seeped through my veins – thick and sweet.

CHAPTER SIX

More Games

"A woman without a man

is like a fish without a bicycle."

Gloria Steinem

G's latest financial offer is so paltry it is obvious he WANTS HIS DAY IN COURT. Writing in capital letters is like SHOUTING.

* * *

I took a photo to my lovely gynaecologist after Colette was born and watched his face fall.

"Ah yes... the photos." He sighed as I rummaged in my bag.

"Not of Colette silly, "you" Post Op looking all 'Man of the Match' I thought it might amuse you but..."

He looked so relieved I fell about laughing. Clearly no one had ever bothered to take one of him before.

He is such a nice man.

Wish I had one.

* * *

Colette smiled so beatifically when I read to her class today. (Expensive London day schools are as short-staffed as the rest it seems.)

* * *

On Wednesday (midweek tea/access) I offer to help Gargoyle buy toiletries for Colette. He gets lost and is late – despite now living round the corner – and looks wild-eyed and desperate on arrival. I smile but he snarls and rushes away to bury my goodwill in the dank garden of his heart, where nothing ever grows.

I try to help him for the sake of Colette and then I leave. He is terrifying.

Six o'clock comes and goes. No sign of Colette. The worry is not will he abscond, but can he even cope with giving her tea once a week?

I make myself wait a bit before telephoning him ('harassing him unreasonably'). Colette is wailing in the background and Gargoyle sounds frantic, so I offer to go over.

"That would be good." He snaps and hangs up. I clearly have to go for Colette's sake... 'And his,' my heart whispers – of course it does, I had married him after all – but in extremis he reveals himself to be the man I left, there is nothing here for me

Hope is very hard to renounce.

CHAPTER SIX

I arrive at the flat, and they look pleased to see me, which is nice. G is jumpy, and I try not to notice the mess and food strewn all over the kitchen surfaces because I do not want to discourage him from asking for help again. Why he does not get a nanny, given all his riches, is beyond me.

He was devastated. Why should he have to get a nanny? Our nanny could have come with me on HIS Wednesdays but LW stopped that. It would have been much easier for me as well to have a familiar face in both places. LW presents herself as the one putting my needs first, but she is completely blind to other people's sensibilities. She behaved as though Dad would bribe the nanny to say nasty things about her in court – clearly ridiculous. One nanny did write a witness statement for the court, I know, but that was different. I can't remember what it was about – presumably to ensure Dad got his rightful access.

When I go into the drawing room, I realise it is not the mess he's jumpy about, but the new Stubbs painting he has forgotten to hide! Quite funny really, when I think about him in court last week banging on about reducing our food budget.

Colette quickly calms down and we play snakes and ladders (somewhat appropriately), although G is so relieved when I arrive he wants me to take her straight home.

I had expected the flat to be full of new toys for Colette, but the Stubbs is the only purchase. The space left by my books has been filled with various silver objets in the same style as a pair of hideous gilt bananas, of which he was always inordinately fond, and which I had 'pinched' (as it felt) from our home when I left, just to tease him. He did not see the joke and was furious, which was pathetically satisfying as he had started being really nasty by then.

* * *

I do try to remember that it is necessarily much more difficult for the person who has been dumped, whether from a dented ego (as in the G's case) or from genuine sorrow.

I consider finding the G some help, but he is still going for sole custody (my friends say it is just a ploy to reduce me to rubble), so I do not because it is not in my legal interests to facilitate his having Colette for long periods when he cannot even cope with the access he already has. He does not really want custody; he just wants to punish me for leaving him because, as he threatened from the start, "If you leave me, I will have Colette taken away from you."

A psychologist recently asked me to draw a picture of myself, and I drew a pile of rubble or rubbish (I do not draw very well).

Unutterably depressing not doing what is best for Colette for fear of legal reprisals.

* * *

Some (wealthy) men do use the courts as a way of coming to terms with being left – litigation is a distraction from reality perhaps – most men are better at anger than sorrow. The G cannot control me any more but he can

CHAPTER SIX

make damn sure I get to court on time.

If you are rich enough, you *can* bully people through the courts, and the G continued to fight for custody even after the finances were settled. Maybe he just missed intimidating me and litigation enabled him to continue terrorising me as he swore he would do unto death.

* * *

I dreamed a strange dream last night, nothing much happened I simply see the ghost of a famous English fashion editor, larger than life, bejeweled, vividly made up and clothed in earthy hues. She is more like a place than a person, so dominant in her physical presence that she becomes her surrounds. Wherever she goes she is the landscape, she is not absorbed into her environment she presides over it. I cannot imagine why she came into my subconscious unless my brain is protecting itself by reverting to memories of happier times.

In the dream, I was a busy fashion journalist so that this English editor had to persuade me to work for her magazine and not one of its competitors. I did not need to fawn over any editors in those heady days when I forgot to remind myself how blessed I was to reside in such an existence. I had blanked my past and the future was tomorrow.

* * *

How it was all to change. How far my guiding star led me away to the soft, grey, not inevitable ashes of disintegration in the guise of an unfortunate choice of mate.

Divorce lends itself to reflection on past mistakes, and you look for any clue that might explain how things came to pass so that you can avoid making the same errors again, and again, I suppose.

* * *

Gargoyle suddenly issues another access order to make it look as though I am currently denying him his access rights (I am not) and then fails to even telephone Colette for a week. I am told to document everything in case I need it for evidence in court. The experience is bad enough without having to catalogue it. This acceleration of acrimony is completely incomprehensible.

* * *

This coming weekend has been 'mine' since we first projected the 'ad hoc' access arrangements until G gets his court order (which he does not need because I have always agreed we should have alternate weekends and Wednesdays and half the holidays and why we need a court order to that effect is beyond me).

Today he suddenly bombards me with demands to have Colette *this* weekend instead of next as had finally been agreed, after protracted legal negotiations. It does not actually matter if he has this weekend instead of next weekend but if I set the precedent whereby he can bully me into changing all arrangements at the 11th hour then he will bully me for evermore. I am unable to make plans with any confidence as it is because there is always the undermining feeling that I do not have the authority to plan things as he may yet come up with a convincing reason as to why I have deliberately messed him around.

CHAPTER SIX

I cannot explain why I am the one who feels continually wrongfooted, probably because I am not messing around but concerned not to organise things for Colette and her friends, which I subsequently have to cancel. G blazes through established routine with no fear of legal consequences let alone the effect on Colette. I am simply left to placate Colette's fury with Mummy ("Daddy says it is all your fault."). If I do not give in to this latest harassment the G's lawyer will use it in court next week as another example of how totally unreasonable I am.

And so it goes on.

When I indicated to Puff that there was a row brewing about this weekend, Puff's response was, "Well let's have the row!" Which is revealing as I realise he does not care about Colette either. Sadly, it is all about fees and 'scoring a point'.

* * *

When G brought Colette back nearly three hours late on Sunday night without telephoning me, I got so frightened I did ring the police and, as I thought, it solved nothing. He went to see them the next day all dressed up in his suit and tie, big shiny car purring outside, a lawyer at his side and that was that. What threat could a rich, white, middle class man possibly pose to society, or more specifically, to his own family?

Money talks and even its subtler notes, if you call a chauffeur subtle, impress.

* * *

My neighbours, Oliver and his girlfriend, were supposed to be coming for dinner with Orson and Lucy last night. Oliver showed up late and alone with some tale about Sara's illness.

Orson thought Oliver leaving his Sara behind was hilarious. "He fancies you and does not want you palling up with his girlfriend! It is not rocket science."

I presume he is right, men are good at spotting each other's agendas.

Lucy recently discovered that Orson has an alternative online life as 'a childless widow whose wife has just died of cancer.'

Aren't men lovely!

* * *

Angela tells me she can't bear to go into the kitchen when she collects her children from G's house on the weekends,

"When you were here there was always food in the fridge."

I smile wryly remembering giving her children tea *every* afternoon. She grew up with a lot of staff but now is reduced to a once a week char and I had become her adopted cook.

Angela and Gargoyle had a row over his next weekend because he can't cope and dumps Colette on her. Angela gets quite heated, "Listen, darling, we all know he is using Colette to torment you. We can all see that he is utterly incompetent!" Angela assures me. She subsequently tells the court I misunderstood what she had said about his incompetence.

Could she not have been just a little more courageous for Colette's sake?

Apparently not.

* * *

An unforgettable vision: Colette getting into G's car with a regal wave, "Bye, bye Mummy," as she swooshes off in the back of the car.

As though she had been doing it all her life...

* * *

We do the first weekend handover at Elizabeth's house to ease the charged atmosphere (which leaves me with tea, sympathy and a stiff whisky post departure as opposed to pacing around peering into Colette's empty bedroom).

The GP says all 'handovers' should be done by someone else, so that Colette is not consumed with guilty feelings of betrayal towards either parent.

* * *

Today, Gargoyle has locked Colette in the car and tells the nanny he will not release her to anyone else but me. I stand outside Starbucks in the rain around the corner from my house shaking so badly from fear and cold that I can't dial for help. I do not know what to do, so I stand beside my car getting drenched in the howling storm. My brain is on fire. I jump so much when my telephone rings that a passing stranger jumps at my fright. The nanny has finally persuaded G to release Colette.

It is over. Colette is home. And safe, at least for now.

'And I was filled with joy...' Colette is singing at the kitchen table as I turn my key in the door, and I rush to bury myself in her softness, which makes her laugh, thrilled by my delight and by my bedraggled state. She thinks it is hilarious, "Wet, Mama, wet, wet!" and laughs.

* * *

I have received yet another document from G's lawyers full of lies and threats. The interim financial arrangements are done for now (although the final settlement was so long in coming I was later advised to go back to court and try to get the temporary arrangements 'uplifted' lest it look as though I could *manage* on a pittance) but the custody battle rages on, a tactic to wear me down so I have no strength left to fight for a decent financial settlement. They say his threats are hollow, but my mind bends and dips in fear.

How can I have married such an appalling person? Everyone must wonder about this because the ghastliness of the process can inspire disgusting behaviour from even mild folk.

Matrimonial lawyers do not help anyone to behave better either.

The lawyers introduce 'chore days' (dental appointments etc) to complicate access arrangements. Time spent with Colette is time spent with Colette, surely?

* * *

CHAPTER SIX

Nigella called last night, "The only point to my life is to have fun," she slurs, "so I drink. You have got a clear point."

To the childless, I am blessed despite the horrors of divorce.

And so I am.

I still finger the Prozac in my pocket longingly on dark days.

* * *

I have decided to take a degree in something to distract me from my domestic dramas. I dread having to look back on the next few years with nothing more to show for myself than a decree absolute. A decree and a degree strike the right note, I think.

Open University. I am reading Portuguese. I applied for Civilisation Studies but that seems to have got lost in translation.

I feel shiny when Randolph arrives. A bottle of Bollinger later and to my horror his mouth is poised to kiss my lips. But my hunger for True Love is not to be assuaged by Old Favourites.

Can turning to Old Favourites really be better than the uncertain comfort of thrilling strangers, I wonder?

I did not try either – doubtless another mistake.

* * *

I telephoned Gargoyle aching to share Colette's glowing school report. Gargoyle's icy response freezes my heart.

I was thinking that because I have left him, he will have become nicer. It is a common mistake; *you* feel better because you have dumped the rubbish so, you expect the rubbish to feel better too.

I left him because he was horrible, and he is still horrible.

Horribler and horribler it seems.

I do not care. I'm going to bed.

* * *

Anna Skips recently saw G at a dinner where he ranted on about my sending out Change of Address cards.

She thought it was a practical move.

"But you are missing the point!" he hissed at her furiously.

The point being that I had got there first with a dignified public announcement.

I knew that would annoy him. How petty we become...

If the worst thing he can come up with is my posting Change of Address cards, he is going to have a tricky time persuading the courts I am an 'unfit' mother.

In the end he just lied and it worked.

BE CAREFUL. ASSUME NOTHING. FIGHT YOUR CORNER.

Judges are often lazy and many are biased towards fathers, assuming all mothers determine to deny their ex-husbands access to their children.

CHAPTER SIX

* * *

Douglas took me to the Ritz on Saturday night. The orchestra struck up and everyone suddenly leapt up to dance and it seemed as though we were in wartime Blighty! The nostalgia soon wore thin; the diners not wartime sweethearts draining their champagne before heading back to the Front after all, but merely tourists having a night out on the town.

Something about the Ritz conjures gentler times – apart from the war thing, obviously.

I cannot imagine ever dancing again. Nothing left of the gay abandon required to throw my limbs about, now. Douglas insists, "it will return, take the anti-depressants. I have seen them work!"

I resist tranquilising my soul.

Douglas declared himself over dinner (again).

Nice to be asked, but he is really quite unsuitable.

* * *

G fails to collect Colette from school for tea. When I ring him, Gargoyle is abusive and says he has never had Colette on Wednesdays despite an (unnecessary) court order issued at his insistence.

Legal missives fly and still Colette hasn't seen her father this week, presumably because he is too busy issuing his sole custody applications. I have to defend myself against the relentless court applications otherwise it will be taken as read that I do not care, whereas G gets (unnecessary) access orders and does not take them up and somehow maintains his status as a devoted father.

Colette and I hopelessly wait for him to collect her for school one morning a week and are late for school when he does not show up, which is used as a black mark against me, "she can't even get her to school on time etcetera..."

* * *

I couldn't have danced all night, but I wish I could have. I wish I could forget. I wish the scorched edges of my mind could be pink and soft again. How do you cut out scarred brain tissue I wonder? Will the slice of a blade make me new and whole and rehabilitate me and my child from all the trauma, when the divorce is absolute?

I force myself to go to a Portuguese tutorial. I am not much of a one for group activities. Some well-meaning nurse once tried selling the idea of antenatal classes to me, and I simply offered her money for a private session. I find this assumed compatibility based on pregnancy, or an interest in Portuguese, absurd. Like being a television presenter; you are pretty, ergo you must be stupid.

The Portuguese students are a dreary lot and the teacher insanely earnest and muttering about children's bed times, I dash off. I will still be using Colette as an excuse to go when she is old and grey.

I worry about my diffidence in the face of strangers and conclude: I am shy and dread being bored.

Colette is adamant, "Daddy says I am going to be with him this weekend. I do not want to go away this weekend, I want to stay with you!"

CHAPTER SIX

I do not know what to do so I stroke her hair.

Children hate being carted around like suitcases. I heard a radio broadcast last week with an eminent psychiatrist speaking against the current Swedish regimen of a split week for 'divorce children'.

"How would you like to move house every four days?" He spits at the so-called expert.

The 'expert' says nothing. Which speaks volumes.

* * *

Some of my friends are questioning their own marriages on the back of my departure. A mistake. When you have to go, you *know*. A change is not necessarily as good as a holiday.

* * *

When Colette is away, I huddle in the playroom watching Barbie movies all weekend.

* * *

Douglas calls me on his way to Toronto. Lucky him.

Everyone else's life looks shiny from the outside.

* * *

92% in my Portuguese exam!

Delirious despite court papers rolling in and no word from Colette all weekend. People say ring the police. What is the point?

I should present the current (excessive) access positively: Wednesday tea, Thursday for breakfast, every other weekend and holidays diced up into alternative weeks.

If things improve, I *should* say, "That was good, but this is terrific."

It is hard.

My complaining about G is damaging and discombobulating for Colette.

I remember years and years of them hating each other. Eventually I hated ***them.***

* * *

Puff says he received a 'letter of outrage' from G because I had changed the locks so he cannot break into my house any more!

My hair falls out in handfuls. It is all grey anyway... so I don't care.

* * *

Colette calls from G's house. It is the first time she has been allowed to. "I'm with Daddy, and I like it," Colette says and goes on to list all the new toys her father has bought for her that day.

Every impoverished, single Mummy knows just how *that* feels.

* * *

CHAPTER SIX

I still find it shaming explaining to strangers that I'm separated. Why, when one in three marriages fail? I assured Colette there would be other divorced children at her new school. There are none. Yet...

By prep school almost everyone was divorced.

* * *

I do not want to go out tonight. I will be flirty, forget I'm not pretty any more, catch my reflection in a mirror and shrivel inside.

I ring Nigella and invite her to come to Elizabeth's party with me (I am determined to show her by example how good friends behave towards each other as well as longing to see her!). She wavers until I throw in a line about 'single men' as that seems to be her only motivation now. She used to be so confident and sassy but now it is all gone, and she seems desperate and drunk most of the time actually.

I catch my cab and reflect on our different attitudes to our current circumstances. My inclination is to share my social life and friends as we used to. Nigella seems to be rather guarded since my return to London. What it is she is guarding is unclear. She knows about Francis, she knows she has nothing to fear. Does she think I made him up? No one I have met since has come near, so she has nothing to fear. I am waiting to feel I have something to offer him other than my divorce woes before I get in touch I suppose though I do not know. I have so little confidence left.

Nigella arrived drunk, I thought, and got drunker. Later she told me she had come straight from some 'meeting' which means she was in a bar before she arrived I suppose. Why she dresses up every drink into a meeting is a source of concern because it makes her seem so insecure (and alcoholic), which I hate. When she goes for a coffee, she calls it a 'meeting'.

* * *

Check up with gynaecologist, whose eyes glisten with tears as I recount proceedings. Kindness when you are on the edge breaks your heart.

I leave the consulting rooms and walk down Harley Street past my old school and imagine the girl I used to be watching the woman I have become, weary and worn by grief and fear.

I retreat to 'Narnis,' the old school café where we used to 'bunk off' for hot chocolates and illicit fags.

Nobody smokes anymore. Bloody heart wrenching (the old school caff not the discarded nicotine habit which is indubitably A Good Thing).

CHAPTER SEVEN

"The world is large, when its weary leagues two loving hearts divide;

But the world is small, when your enemy is loose on the other side."

John Boyle O'Reilly, *Distance*

Colette's deputy head tells me that Gargoyle has just been in to explain 'the situation'. I gape.

I did not ask the deputy head what G termed 'the situation' and assume she now thinks I am as awful as he says (unlikely as most schools have, as Colette's headmistress subsequently assures me kindly, "seen it all before"). I am appalled. So shaming.

G badgers my friends, hangs around school, and drives slowly beside us throwing out comments to Colette as we walk to school. Really sinister, but I do not tell anyone because they would not believe me.

* * *

Some people never get the knack of not being frightened and sad, according to the radio.

* * *

This morning my neighbour helps me unload the groceries, "It was rather quiet in your house on Sunday. I thought your ex- must have come in and murdered you all."

Blimey.

CHAPTER EIGHT

"Nobody Loves a Fairy When She's Forty"
Arthur W D Henley, song title

I note how pathetic I have become about face creams recently, just another fortysomething-year-old sucker looking for a fix. So convinced am I by the notion that high-end face creams are more effective that I now know exactly how much I must spend in order to save my face, which is absurd. As anyone who has worked in the fashion business knows perfectly well, you are paying for the advertising and branding not the actual cream. I know all this, but still...

Only human, I suppose. Anyway I pay £525 for face balm. Hope it works!

* * *

I tell Colette I am lonely as the post thuds onto the carpet. Colette takes my hand and smiles, "I'm your friend, Mummy, talk to me."

Beautiful child.

I have no recollection of this and wish she would come home.

* * *

I bump into Tim and Alex and Alex asks, "Are you using Ray?" assuming that as the 'disgruntled wife of a rich man', Raymond Tooth, matrimonial lawyer to the rich and famous, must be my lawyer. Divorce is such a singular journey that you only relate to people in the same boat, which makes for a grim stretch of river actually.

"I do not mind that my ex-husband took all my dough, but the exhaustion of the process destroyed my last good years," Alex says.

I still thought that a good night's sleep would make me look nice again and felt a tiny bit smug about not being in quite the same boat. Another mistake.

I was eventually forced to concede the permanence of my caved in face, and the nervous disposition that means I still jump every time the telephone rings and hold my breath when the post hits the floor; legal documents, threats and court papers all take their toll.

* * *

Tim takes me aside at a party, bewailing his break-up with Alex. He feels old (depressing as we are the same age), poor and past it. Reassurances flow from my lips, "You are young, handsome, famous and successful – you will find someone else."

People say this sort of thing to me a lot and it helps.

We share a taxi after the party and, as I get out, Tim beams, "You made my evening. Thank you."

I feel exhilarated and humbled, because he really *is* a catch, and it is nice to feel I still have something to offer people too.

I feel shelf-weary when he remarries eight months later. I am still knee-deep in affidavits.

I will find *my* Prince (I have found my Prince – I just need to ring him up).

* * *

I offer to make Gargoyle a picnic for the park, hoping to make things nicer for Colette. He thanks me and departs muttering about all the meals he has to cook and the shopping he hasn't done for their weekend. He is a rich man who can afford to pay staff but is determined to get a court order to let him use my nanny. Puff says, "Everything is about money. He thinks he is paying for her and so is entitled to use her on his access days."

Nothing about making things better for Colette.

Why can she not understand Dad probably thought it would be nicer if I had a familiar face in both places.

I have escaped his controlling clutches, so I try to step back, but when I look into his eyes I see all his malice and the years of misery it has caused.

I am worried about Colette and hope people are rallying round. And then I guess he'll fix himself up permanently (with his secretary as it transpires), and then I will be annoyed!

Dad's secretary wore a lot of makeup, I did not like her sticky kisses. I do not remember anything else about her.

G says my picnic sandwiches were a bore because Colette loved them and wanted more.

A simple 'Thanks' would have been fine.

God, what a nightmare, even cucumber sandwiches are an emotive topic. Ugh.

* * *

Randolph says it is easier to go off the rails if you are alone during the divorce process. He was worrying about his ex-wife ever finding someone new. She is spectacularly hideous so I can see the problem. I am having trouble enough ridding myself of the one I have got to be unduly disturbed by future relations.

I do not want to ring Francis until my life is less sordid. I have nothing to offer. I feel needy, which is not attractive.

* * *

Randolph (whose ex-wife will not complete her Form E either), explains that FDR stands for Financial Dispute Resolution. Essentially you go to court, argue about money and the judge *indicates* what the settlement will *probably* be in a final hearing. You can then negotiate with 'the other side' in the corridor. The majority of divorces settle at this stage.

Mine did not.

Proceeding with court lines the lawyers' pockets, leaving their clients impoverished and furious.

CHAPTER EIGHT

* * *

I do not contact Francis.

* * *

Dear Florence is having breast implants; Botox injected into her face, knees and ankles; liposuction on her bottom; and is taking a course of drugs to enhance her suntan. What is wrong with diet, exercise and a sun lounger?

Nigella, also single, has joined a supper club, where each girl brings a man she does not fancy. A bunch of spinsters pooling a herd of rejects!

Oh dear.

Supper with Thomas, lovely until he inevitably mulls the mystery of why we aren't lovers, and I resist shrieking, "Because I do not fancy you!"

He picks up that I am financially embarrassed and arrives with an envelope the next morning, "I thought you might prefer cash, so you can pay me back whenever you can and no one will know." He knows I have to sign endless updated Form E's and a sudden injection of thousands of pounds from a male friend might not read well in court.

He made it as light as a fiver between friends when he must have known what it cost me to accept.

Seamless gold. Some people never recover from the terror of financial straits. I still tingle when I make large payments, although I am ok now.

Florence is in love with the boy in the video shop downstairs. They spend their time kissing in the back of the car in the Bois de Boulogne. Apparently the windows completely steamed up last time. She is getting tired of rushing between lives and talks of divorce.

I could not cope with the guilt and I cannot lie for nuts but her husband is only dull not nasty. It is a bigger step than she imagines from inside her steamy bubble.

* * *

My current mantra, 'remember, it is fury that drives him to such lengths and not some Pilgrims' Progress Slough of Despond I must endure because I have committed moral outrage.'

I have not been judged and found wanting by any higher power; I have left a man and dented his pride.

* * *

I get a text on my way to school this morning saying, "You are evil."

I was so horrified that I deleted it immediately never thinking how useful such proof of abuse might have been. I hate mobiles. It feels like a suppurating slug periodically excreting pus, that I am obliged to carry around in my handbag.

The elation I experience every time that I hear a message come in, steel myself to face the putrid excrement and find to my relief that it is not from him, is pathetic.

And exhausting.

* * *

CHAPTER EIGHT

Decree nisi arrives with *another* custody petition.

* * *

Randolph admits it suits him not to have his daughter for prolonged periods because there are limited things for him to do with his daughter. Even super dads are viewed with suspicion by mummies.

Randolph accepts his ex-wife as primary carer and bows to her demands for the sake of their child.

I had forgotten how sexist my mother could be. She nattered to her girlfriends, and I listened at doors in the hallucinogenic hope of hearing her say nice things about Dad and because I was anxious about the possibility of another seismic upheaval in my life.

I was married to the Gargoyle for 12 years before I left him. I tried everything to avoid separation: talking, marriage guidance, etc. The day Colette came home astonished at finding that other people's parents shared a room, I knew the time had come to leave.

Time to leave...

* * *

I am flirting with the purchase of a cat.

Nigella thinks it is a marvellous idea.

Elizabeth disapproves. "Absolutely not. It is the thin end of the wedge!"

So that's that then.

* * *

I complained about the viciousness of my divorce today, and Tom crushingly quipped, "Is there any such thing as an amicable divorce?"

Books telling us how civilised divorce can be tend to be written by happily married people.

Or liars.

* * *

Today is official midweek tea day with Daddy again.

I hold my breath all afternoon (again) and finally telephone G at 6.30pm to hear Colette screaming in the background. I offer to go round and help (again) and he readily agrees (again).

As we were all sitting in G's kitchen, Colette calm now, I heard someone's key turning in the lock. I peer round the kitchen door and nearly fall off my seat when the pretty blonde who serves me my cappuccino at the local café every day, breezes in.

"Eva!" I exclaimed.

She took one look at me and dived deep into her bag busying herself in it for as long as it took G to bluster something about, "Eva comes round to do a bit of this and that occasionally."

"This and that..." I mused aloud, leaving the phrase hanging in the air a while.

It was beautiful.

CHAPTER EIGHT

Eva finally stood up to face me and, thrusting forward some sweeties she had apparently brought for Colette, she hurriedly scuttled back from whence she came – my local cafe as it happens.

Every time I think of the expression on her face (and Gargoyle's) it makes me smile and smile. Delicious.

* * *

Eva is predictably sheepish when I collect my coffee today and, as I am paying, she unexpectedly asks me if I will write a reference for her as she is looking for a new job. I nearly spit my cappuccino over her shirt in amazement. Choking the hot coffee back down my throat, I draw myself up to my full height so that I am now towering above her and languidly drawl,

"Eva as you are clearly fucking my ex-husband, I suggest you ask him for a reference."

With which I swept forth into the street, almost colliding with G who was on his way in.

Time to find a new coffee spot I think.

* * *

Nigella says G will rapidly replace me because, "Men cannot cope alone once they have been married."

G's going for a shared residency order (as well as sole custody) now, which the lawyers say is meaningless as both parents automatically share custody, but then why is he bothering?

Hmm. Well I think I can imagine fighting on if there were the smallest possibility that I would get my child back. He loved me; why cannot she accept that he loved me… in his own way?

James says Gargoyle just wants to frighten me (it is working), "You will not lose custody of your child, and you will get some money and somewhere to live permanently. The rest is psychological warfare."

I ask G to take Colette back to school after the school concert. He agrees and then takes Colette out for the afternoon!

Puff says, "We must do a letter straight away. This sort of thing results in children becoming drug addicts."

My stomach lurches. I cannot breathe. The sun is eclipsed. Real fear.

The lawyers wind you up so that you agree to ineffectual, *expensive* 'letters of outrage' (as they are known in the trade).

* * *

I wish Puff would not ring at night with bad news, or on a Friday dealing some devastating blow before clocking off for the weekend, leaving me with no one to talk to and on overdrive until daybreak, when hopefully a friend will rescue me from the ghouls.

Puff's latest advice is, "There's a 'scene' at your club you know… Marriages break up…"

I have no idea what he is talking about until I suddenly realise that he is warning me to resist sleeping with my tennis coach!

How desperate do I look?

* * *

Colette is away with G for half-term. No financial settlement reached. I lack the means (and volition) to go anywhere. The custody battle drags on with the usual 'salami-slicing' of Colette's time. I hear nothing, as usual (the silence allows the furies to infect my mind and twist me out of shape from within). Catatonic, I sit by the door until Colette rushes in and wriggles into my arms.

G takes 20 minutes to transport belongings from the boot and drives off, only to return minutes later pushing random items of Colette's clothing through the letterbox and bellowing through its narrow slit disparaging comments about how Colette would be better off if she never saw me again – which inevitably makes Colette fretful and angry (with me).

G often posts things through the door at night, so I find sinister evidence of his nocturnal lurking when I drag myself downstairs in the morning, dreading some further outpouring of venom or yet another court summons.

CHAPTER NINE

"A belief in a supernatural source of evil is not necessary; men alone are quite capable of every wickedness."

Joseph Conrad, *Under Western Eyes*

Linda's is the first face I see as I enter the health club changing rooms today. She looks as beautiful as the last time I saw her (approximately 15 years ago on a *Vogue* shoot).

Did I sit in the front row watching her on the catwalks of Paris and Milan, or have I gone mad?

We chat a little until I unwittingly catch sight of my own face in the mirror, and any self-confidence I might ever have possessed, seeps down through my toes into the cracks in the floor.

I long for a black hole to swallow me up. Would not take more than a pothole: two dress sizes down and still shrinking.

If I do not bounce back post-divorce, I will take a long look at the blade of the surgeon's knife.

* * *

This morning I drowsily snuggled up to an empty space where Colette usually nestles from early morning. It must take time for her to get used to it too.

* * *

I am not ready to find Francis because I do not know if I'm any wiser than I was. What if my taste is still faulty? He might turn out to be another monster.

I receive a marvellous letter from a rich friend, who majestically dismisses my change of name and address on my new cards by saying,

"I guess I'm behind with the news,"

Before cataloguing the seismic upheaval caused by her cleaner's departure.

The rich are different...

Musing about shoulders I once leant on and then find I cannot think of any! Hilarious. Or not.

I dreamed of having interrupted sex with Bob Geldof last night. The interrupted part I get, it is the Bob Geldof bit I do not understand!

I laugh out loud, her taste in men seems pretty sound to me.

I shall end up like Betjeman whose only regret was wishing he'd "had more sex."

Two years of court battles. People say G will get bored, but he will not; he has got nothing else to do and his determination to punish me blinds him to the damage he wreaks on Colette.

I put down the diary. She sounds sad.

* * *

Henry's 40th birthday party: I was propositioned by a couple, and it took a long time for me to understand that they were committed to threesomes.

Is this what single life heralds?

* * *

Odd conversation with Billy, who was offended when I said his first wife was grumpy. "She was not grumpy," he snapped.

Refreshing to hear someone defend their ex.

CHAPTER TEN

"Indifferent the finches sing,
Unheeding roll the lorries past:
What misery will this year bring
Now spring is in the air at last?"

Sir John Betjeman, *Loneliness*

Today I seem to have found resonance in a bit of Aeschylus, *"The inexorable pain of living from which we can choose to learn or not but from which pain we cannot escape."*

Obviously a good day then!

I do not think I had a hangover though because the wine's always so filthy at Henry's parties I do not drink, something to do with him having had a rather grand champagne-fuelled childhood has led him to conclude that cheap Greek wine is 'edgy.'

The rest of us just think that it is brain pain.

Had a big whisky when I got home after the party as usual in the hallucinogenic hope of slumber, which rarely comes. Comforting though with honey and lemon and hot water.

* * *

I receive a hideous financial offer from G, and Randolph comes to Puff's office with me as I have lost the plot. It helps.

It is a good idea to take a friend to see your lawyer if you get bogged down by the detail.

I must remember this is a financial negotiation, not a personal evaluation of me as a wife and mother.

But it still makes me shake with fury and terror. Might we really end up with nowhere to live and nothing to live on? Anyway, why is G crunching the numbers and not paying attention to Colette?

The only way to survive this horrible business is to try to see it for what it is: a row about money. I am desperate to savour the time with Colette while she is still little because everyone says from the moment children are born "enjoy them now, blink and they're grown."

"When your children are babies you love them so much you want to eat them all up, and when they are bigger... you wish you had!" (Spanish proverb)

I never got the chance.

CHAPTER ELEVEN

"Who would have thought my shriveled heart
Could have recovered greenness?"
George Herbert, *The Flower*

Francis

I ring Francis and he rings me back. It is one of the happiest memories of my life.

I gaily invite him (and his wife) to my birthday supper.

"Oh I am afraid it would just be me though, and I will be a bit late as I have to go to an event before," he said and I danced all the way to Colette's school.

"Heaven's grinning, me and the birds are singing, Mummy's gone potty and we all fall down." I dance and sing around Colette while she eats her tea.

* * *

The beginning of my Annabel's evening feels like a dream. So much has happened since then: I remember getting ready, putting on my new Gucci gown, long and elegant and a hideous shade of green, times are quite hard and the gown was massively reduced (for obvious reasons I think as I contemplate myself in the bathroom mirror – which does have unkind lights – so maybe it is not as bad as it seems).

Nigella arrives to escort me to my soiree, and she is so enthusiastic and lovely as she has become again; full of ambition and expectations for her future and it is always so exciting to be around her, and her tremendous energy makes everything such fun.

She rings my doorbell long and hard and when I open it, I find her dressed in a shiny burgundy sheath of a dress with masses of makeup and mascara dripping down to her chin because she has plastered it on so heavily, as is her wont. She appears shining out of the night as I go to greet her, like a fairy godmother arriving with the carriage to whisk me off to my night in the stars. She is larger than life and glorious, a triumph of clashing colours and enthusiasm over taste. No one else can put things together the way she does and look good, but she carries it off because her dress sense is purely a reflection of her joyous character.

She immediately starts babbling away and we tumble into the back of the waiting taxi admiring each other's gowns and figures and hair as we always do (even when we are feeling hideous). She has such a talent still for conjuring glittering balls in the air, out of nothing really so that even a cup of tea with her is a treat I look forward to with a real smile knowing she will lift me up and make everything seem colourful and gay.

She is the very best friend a girl could have.

CHAPTER ELEVEN

We scramble out of the taxi and descend into the basement club and within minutes all my guests arrive and we are drinking champagne, nibbling sushi and talking rubbish at one another the way one does at these things.

I was shaking with excitement and I could not hear a thing anyone said to me because all I could think about was would Francis still be the same? Would I still be so enthralled that my hairs stand on end? Would every word he utters still make my flesh prickle with excitement and a sort of terror that he might suddenly stop and go away? I have only met him once, but sometimes that is enough.

All I cared about was that Francis would come, and I would find him as absorbing and exhilarating as I had done that one evening all those years ago.

We eventually made our way through the throng and music of the club to the central dining table where I had placed a man either side of me. I tucked Francis's place card behind mine so that I could slip it out on his arrival and reshuffle someone else. The plan was simply to throw the dullest man away and supplant him with Francis when he arrived. Not a very gracious plan but wholly forgivable in the circumstances I decided.

As always the club was full on a Thursday night and I was delighted, everyone likes going to Annabel's because it is a rare treat, as you have to be a member or, as in my case, kindly granted dispensation by the owner. Actually, even giving dinners at Annabel's is a nightmare though because people are so unreliable that you are invariably scrabbling around on the morning of the event dredging up old friendships from long discarded address books in the hope of finding suitable last-minute stand-ins. Extraordinary how ill-mannered people are though, perhaps because so few people host dinner parties any more they have no idea how trying it is to be told at the eleventh hour that you are now a man or girl short. So as usual, despite the wow factor of the glamorous club it still was in those days, several people had let me down and flowers and gifts had been arriving in some form or another throughout the week, whether in apology for not being able to make it, or in pointed gratitude at being asked at so late a date and therefore so obviously from the 'B list'. I did not care.

All that mattered to me was that there were enough people to camouflage my singular interest in a man who, it was reasonable to presume, had not a clue who I was or why he had been asked and was therefore only coming out of curiosity – but in my heart I did not really believe that at all!

I was exhilarated and careless of my surroundings that night waiting only for him. I had my back to the entrance, but I knew I would know the moment he arrived.

"I'll count to three and turn around and there he'll be. And if I know him immediately, and the world turns for me, then there will be no doubt that he is no mere fantasy born of a sad girl lost in hell county," I told myself.

It all played out as I had predicted: one minute chattering and simultaneously nodding at a waiter to refill my glass

CHAPTER ELEVEN

and then a sudden lurching of my stomach as I felt Him come in.

And thus I was able to finish my sentence, fluidly rise, and turn in time to take his arm and greet him just as he approached our table.

And all the lights were blazing, and there was no doubt he was the Beloved and not some faint dream. The feelings were all as they had been. Here he was, the man I have thought of every day since our first encounter. We met years ago and there was nothing to sustain me other than an unyielding certainty that we are a pair in some unspecific dimension.

He stood there twinkling and presented me with a heavy bag of gifts, "You said it was your birthday."

I took his arm in mine and began introducing him to the others around the table and then suddenly I simply gave up and sat us down. I only wanted him, and he did not seem to mind at all, just smiled, accepted a drink, and made me feel as if I was the only girl in the world by the intensity with which he looked at and spoke to me.

Later, as planned, I allowed myself to be distracted by Randolph who was sitting on my other side, so that Elizabeth, who was strategically placed, could ask Him all sorts of questions and probe him in a way that would be wholly unsuitable for me to do.

He did not stand a chance, not really, although I did not see it like that then.

When Elizabeth had finished with him, so to speak, we returned to each other and that was it. I was not going to let conventional manners interrupt us again, not when I had waited so long. Every nerve was alert to the realisation that at last I had found my right mooring.

We planned voyages across continents, oh a whole future we mapped out that birthday evening. I did not want it to end. I held hard and fast to every single second of him. We grew wings and flew. Everything we touched upon ignited another spark of excitement at the complicity between us. We fused as one and we fizzed away all evening.

So electrifying that even Snooksey, who was miles away at the other end of the long table, came over to us just as we were crossing the Atlantic in high winds and crouching down beside us, he smiled up and started joining in, "You two are obviously planning magnificent voyages to exotic lands one can just see, where have you got to now, High Winds of Jamaica?"

It was pleasing to note our enthusiasm for one another was so apparent to all that it made them want to come in. No room at the inn but delicious to know how pervasive happiness can be.

The only funny footnote I cannot resist recording is me and Elizabeth snatching a quiet moment together in what is known as 'The Buddha Room' as she was leaving and how, trembling with excitement, I quizzed her as to what she thought of him (I made a bad choice of husband, and I was longing for some reassurance, despite everything I thought I knew), and Elizabeth simply stated, "A different league to anyone you have ever known, my dear."

I kicked my heels together with glee, until a dull thought dropped me down to earth with a thud, "I have not had sex for years, what if I cannot remember how to do it?" I wailed to Elizabeth.

"It is like riding a bike, sweetheart, once you have mastered the art you do not fall off."

I hope she is right, my bike's been in the shed for A Very Long Time.

"He is definitely keen, so I hope you are sure?" she advised as she stood up to go, giving me an outrageous wink. She can be very naughty.

In my book 'keen' means no delay or not much anyway, and certainly not more than the woman concerned wants there to be! In short, I assumed we would make love that evening because nothing would hold me back; why should it? I have waited so long, and I am so sure. It seemed inevitable.

We did not, but it was lovely. Magical man. He brought me home and we kissed passionately for hours. Literally. I understand the kissing thing now. Never have before. It was like an ethereal rehearsal for making love and more, more, more! But he is cautious (and Catholic, bit alarming as I think adultery might be a mortal sin, but not sure – must check with Elizabeth), and married, so of course we did not, could not. But we will. Inevitably. Eventually.

It was novel and pleasantly liberating to find myself being, for once, the one who wanted more than the man of the moment was prepared to offer. I think he might have been a bit taken aback by my wild enthusiasm. Understandably, given how I had thrown myself into his arms on the dance floor and stuck to his lips like glue all night long.

Poor man.

CHAPTER TWELVE

"All days are nights to see till I see thee,
And nights bright days when dreams do show thee me."

William Shakespeare, Sonnet 43

Francis telephones and we arrange to meet. I go to Prada for a dress because I have to feel confident and a Prada dress will help.

I lose my nerve and tell Elizabeth I'm going to cancel.

"Why would you do that? Games will frighten him."

"I do not want him to think I'm completely desperate!"

She just fell about laughing. "But darling you are... completely bloody desperate, and it is sweet. Don't you think he is terrified too? He has more to lose than you."

I crumpled and she took pity,

"Oh Cecily, darling, I know you love him terribly and so on…"

I wish she would stop reducing my agony to "and so on".

When you are *consumed* with someone, you are terrified of rejection.

I show the Prada. I look nice. I must go.

* * *

Supper.

"If it were only myself I had to consider, I would marry you tomorrow," he says, grasping my hands.

I breathe and he smiles, enveloping me in all his humble longing and a waiter arrives.

Oh she sounds so happy.

I did not know until that moment that he had understood me at all.

He was bewildered and at the same time bowled over, not quite as in control as he is used to being, I suppose. That he was unable to prevent himself from responding to me, despite his terrors, is all the encouragement I need.

We ate, or more accurately we ordered, he ate and I watched him happily munching away. Not unselectively guzzling but really relishing good things. He is very childlike I think. When it is good he tucks in and when it is finished he looks for pudding. That was lovely.

"Please sir, I want some more"!

You can tell a lot about people from the way they eat.

My stomach was busy with butterflies, so I sipped his carefully chosen wine – I could not decide on red or white so he solved it by ordering some of each – and watched him being happy and me glowing and growing in confidence because he was happy with me.

CHAPTER TWELVE

He brought me home and accepted my offer to come in. "Just for a moment, I have a lot of work to finish so I mustn't be late... but a cup of coffee would be lovely."

So I gave him a brandy and dragged him up to my room, brazen hussy that I am, or seem to be, in the face of Cautious Catholics. I have not encountered such restraint in a man before; it is impressive but undaunting because it will come right. When he feels safe it will come right... and not before.

I instinctively know the most important thing for him is to arrive in his own time. I can feel how poised for flight at the slightest fright he is. If he could he would persuade himself that he is imagining all and that it is but a fleeting fancy on my part, he would disappear. He was resigned to be being lonely until I came along and he had not expected me at all I think. He has a guilty secret, some misdemeanor of the past, and so he deserves nothing more, only to be punished by moral guilt, he thinks.

You really can tell a lot about people from the way they eat!

* * *

I telephone Nigella as soon as I wake up and tell her all in a garbled mess, but she seems to get the basic outline of the plot and observes, to my admiration, because it is very hard to see things about yourself which are often obvious to outsiders, that the dynamic in our relationship is inverted so that I am the seducing male in the face of Francis's feminine resistance. I had not thought of it like that, but she is right. There is a role reversal, which suits both of us actually as I generally dread being pursued – not in this instance obviously – as much as he clearly dreads the guilt and responsibility of taking things further.

I know he will not be in touch for weeks because the only way he can allow himself to have me in his life at all is by pretending that we are just casual friends and there is no danger after all.

He must have had to steel himself from reaching for the telephone with as much force as I needed to bear his absences in those first months. (I know he did because when he did call it was erratic and always with some caveat that I "might need some help".)

* * *

My three oldest friends sit in the kitchen trashing men. I hug my knees to my chest in blissful contentment and pounce on my telephone when it burbles and winks.

It is the love you *know* will come when you are young and have given up on by the time you are twenty-five.

Or, until you realise it will probably end in divorce.

The first time Francis asks, "Why do you like me so much?"

I say, "I'm desperate!"

We laugh. A lot.

Ridiculous.

CHAPTER THIRTEEN

"How can I then return in happy plight,
That am debarred the benefit of rest,
When day's oppression is not eased by night,
But day by night and night by day oppressed,
And each, though enemies to either's reign,
Do in consent shake hands to torture me,
The one by toil, the other to complain
How far I toil, still farther off from thee?"

William Shakespeare, *Sonnet 28*

It is the freshest of blades that slides inside as I watch Colette's little head moving away from me with sorrowful step today.

"Bye, bye my darling, I love you," I cry after her, but she barely turns and is soon caught up in the melee of children arriving at school. And then I remember that it is Wednesday and the dread of horrifying handovers floods my mind with apprehension.

I want to lie in the snow with peaceable flakes settling over me, touched only by deathly cold and nothingness.

Colette is supposed to be home at 6pm. I sit on the bed counting the minutes, trying to convince myself that I am not counting the minutes.

* * *

My father snatched a sibling and reached the Italian border before he was arrested, and my brother realised they were not having an adventure but breaking the law.

* * *

We could be having a lovely time planning Christmas together for Colette.

I have offered him unlimited access and yet he spits, "It is not in your gift to offer it!"

Mad.

* * *

Colette says, "You should sue them, Mummy!" if something goes wrong, presumably because we constantly go to court. Litigation has become a way of life to her now; it is the knee jerk response to being thwarted. This is what we, her parents, are teaching her. We are not doing a good job.

* * *

It is helpful to get a male take on things occasionally because girlfriends' outrage only exacerbates my own feelings.

* * *

G is going to court to get his Christmas dates.

CHAPTER THIRTEEN

James says I have been badly advised (by a paediatrician) not to defend myself in court. He is right. But I do not go because it is bad for Colette, who always knows, how can she not, when her parents are at it again.

G gets all the dates he wants and costs against me because I am not there to rebut his lies.

CHAPTER FOURTEEN

*"I teach you the superman.
Man is something to be surpassed."*
Friedrich Nietzsche (1844-1900)

Gargoyle collected Colette from a school netball match unannounced today and left me waiting outside the school gates in the freezing cold, for an hour and a half, until the headmistress came out and said that all the other pupils had returned a long time ago. I did not know what to do other than wait, I explained, as G was not answering his telephone.

"I will call his lawyer – come inside it is starting to snow."

She made the call and they eventually showed up, Colette screaming and kicking and accusing me of constantly calling the police against Daddy. I tried to stay calm it is not her fault. I suggested she might like to go and have tea with her friend down the road thinking it was better for her to go to a clean environment where she could forget about her troubles and be an ordinary little girl having her tea and playing with someone else's toys.

I am watching the tragedy of my child's life unfolding and I cannot rescue her. I will always be blamed because as Colette hisses, "We were happy and you smashed everything." Because that is what she is told.

The price is higher than I could have imagined.

CHAPTER FIFTEEN

"It makes the wounded spirit whole,

And calms the troubled breast;

'Tis manna to the hungry soul,

And to the weary rest."

Olney Hymns (1779) 'How sweet the name of Jesus sounds'

I have not heard from Francis for a long time. If I do not stir, he will assume I do not care, so I send a silly text, "Phone sex? Just kidding. Sleep tight."

Seconds later I hear a ping, "Are you still awake?"

"Even I cannot do phone sex asleep."

He, "Call me?" he asks and of course I oblige. The sound of his voice thrills and calms me. He is clever and wise (and still managing to delude himself that everything he does is for me).

We spoke for three hours and it was wonderful and when the morning came, I had not slept and all felt bleak because our relationship has not actually progressed, we have just had another silly conversation, that is all.

Nothing!

* * *

I like the Lord Denning "clarity of thought inexorably leading to clarity of language" beguiling notion that there is a system to distinguish and uphold justice. *Do not* be beguiled. Judges' decisions are, on the whole, pretty arbitrary.

Court dates loom in such quantity that the inclination to invest in fur and pearls for a full high court hearing becomes compelling, and I visit the local charity shop to buy the goods.

"How could I have chosen such an appalling father for Colette?" I mutter after a recent court appearance as we are all climbing into a taxi for the dreary ride home (in silence – it did not go well).

"That is the mystery for us all, Cecily," Puff grumbles sotto voce.

* * *

Dinner at San Lorenzo with three would-be divorcees. One was funny and shocking about the naughty things she did to keep her husband from playing 'away' games. Once they were married, he took up with her best friend whom he is now proposing to marry, expecting my friend to 'join in' and put up with a *menage a trois*. She was not unduly surprised because *she* had been the best friend of his first wife.

I was quite shocked, but she said it all so naturally that it made me feel like a prude. Is this really perfectly acceptable behaviour?

Could she reapply for the vacant mistress position? I wondered. She already had! (Nowt so queer as folk, I suppose.)

Everyone else's husband is offering reasonable access and financial settlements whereas G orders me to apply for State Benefits (which I get, but know I will have to repay post-settlement when I will no longer qualify. I listen to *The Money Programme* on Radio 4 sometimes, which is full of odd nuggets about this sort of thing). I am effectively being forced to eat into capital I do not yet have, so my settlement is diminished before it has arrived, as the G well knows.

A nasty little swipe, I cannot help thinking.

When the bill arrives, I have to borrow money from one of the girls. San Lorenzo is a cash only establishment.

* * *

Yet another access hearing, and Puff tells me that this judge sometimes talks to the respective parties in the absence of lawyers. Cafcass (welfare) aren't always available. Today we are lucky.

Mr Cafcass is handsome, articulate, and tweedy! He fails to convince G not to litigate when we have not had time to detach our feelings for each other from what is best for Colette.

The judges want you to get on with each other for the sake of your children.

My barrister urges me to continue to offer mediation for the record. The courts frown on litigants who do not *try* to settle.

G agrees to mediate on condition that he can continue to litigate *simultaneously*!

This 'conciliation' costs thousands with nothing agreed, other than to come back "At Risk." Which I thought meant that Colette was to be put on the At Risk Social Services list. My lawyer explains that it actually means you show up on a given day and hang around the court hoping somebody does not show up and you get their slot.

The judge, having heard our statements, tells us when to come back for a judgment but encourages us to try to reach an agreement between ourselves in the interim so that another appearance will not be necessary.

Fat chance, I mumble to myself. He has no idea what I am dealing with.

G wanted blood... at any cost. Half a million so far!

Wow!

Gargoyle thinks that squeezing me financially, and threatening to take Colette away, will force me to go back to him and there have been low days when I have been tempted. G uses Colette as a weapon because it is the easiest way to soften me up for a lousy financial settlement.

Men are better at differentiating between bullying tactics (which I do not employ anyway) and actual danger. For example, if your child has nits you will not lose custody, no matter how many letters of outrage your ex-husband writes about it, but if you are a deranged alcoholic you could and should risk losing custody of your child.

I'm eager to get to high court and settle all these issues once and for all (in my favour of course). Puff has a deal of experience with arbitrary judgments though and is suddenly unexpectedly keen to impress upon me that 'nothing is in the bag' despite Gargoyle's recent antics (which Puff has been reassuring me until now, will negatively impact on his sole custody demands). G thinks he has right on his side because *I* left him. I think G is behaving like a lunatic and Colette, who is still very young, needs the stability of her mummy as primary carer, as I have been hitherto. Impasse.

The high court judge will therefore decide.

* * *

The lawyers encourage the 'dream team' fallacy, but there is no 'DT' there is me now negotiating a bank loan to pay my lawyers, who are snapping at my heels for money on account. I do not find Puff's comment that "it is no bad thing for you to be able to show the court that you have been placed heavily into debt by your legal fees" particularly uplifting either.

Francis

Francis arrives and I race to the door, my *sangfroid* discarded with my knickers. I require so little and these snatched moments of passion keep me going for weeks.

* * *

I am crouching in the tall grass, attuned to every rustling that might herald another wave of malevolence. The waves drag me down airless depths and dump me in dark corners of my psyche.

Endless legal conferences and exchanges of dreary, 'Without Prejudice' paltry offers and interminable impenetrable documents fill waking moments.

* * *

I fall asleep on top of Colette during her bedtime story, and she gently eases herself out from under me, as I discover next morning, and curls up to sleep on the (heated) bathroom floor. "You were so tired, Mama," she says, sketching great rings under my eyes.

I read about a fellow who, finding himself in the presence of Princess Diana, performed a deep curtsey! Princess Diana clapped her hands exclaiming, "Again, again!"

I find myself giggling uncontrollably.

Good to laugh.

CHAPTER SIXTEEN

*"We are prepared to go
to the gates of Hell –
but no further."*

Pope Pius VII

(on attempting to reach agreement with Napoleon)

Francis arrives after a long absence. Abandoning 'us' is impossible after all.

God why don't they just get on with it?

This most recent brandishing of his steel heart in self-exile has been his most determined effort to escape me/us so far. That evening we tacitly acknowledged that he has tried to say goodbye and is now conceding defeat, albeit in some distant future. That the longing and loving has been whispered, is enough for now. Oh, but his hesitant sensitivity imbues in me the patience of a saint.

* * *

A few days later I get a text: "*dove?*" And I delayed responding as I thought he was talking in clever code and could not come up with what I considered a suitably witty response. I eventually made do with answering, "pigeon" (message carrier) and when it transpired he was talking Italian (where are you?) and not clever code at all we both laughed so much the tears ran down my face. So worried about making a fool of myself I make a complete goose and utter idiot of myself and then after all it is lovely and funny.

* * *

He draws me in, and as soon as one is reassured the other is happy. The pleasure of the gift becomes one's own present to unwrap, leisurely and lovingly.

He calls me on his way home, "How are you?"

I make an explosive noise, signifying pent up passion unspent.

"I know, like getting on a jet plane and going home in the tube."

His prosaic analysis of a wealth of unspeakable, muddle and joy.

* * *

I wake up to a bleak day and go to Lincoln's Inn to see a tax barrister.

Real life trudges on.

If you remain a secret too long, you lose a sense of self.

* * *

Francis telephones to ask me what I am doing. "A car has just drawn up outside my door and there is a man carrying a present getting out," I say provocatively.

"Coming towards you?"

"Seems to be." I laugh.

"Have a lovely evening," he says.

"That is not the required response!" I admonish, "You are supposed to be *green* and horrified."

He chuckles so delightedly that I imagine his eyes twinkling in mirth as he demands with faux fury, "Who is this cad? I demand to know. How long have you known him and what does he want?"

"That's it, that's better," I say.

Gales of laughter.

CHAPTER SEVENTEEN

"A contract which binds me without putting you under any obligation is unfair, I must decline."
Stendhal, *Le Rouge et Le Noir*

How did I manage with so little to go on? Well there was plenty of divorce to distract me, and I determinedly recorded it because I wished someone had written something for me to refer to when things got nasty. Having some idea of what to expect would have helped… a lot.

A long time ago Colette watched me chattering to Francis and wailed, "Mummy why can't you look so shiny and excited when *I* talk to you?"

Court

Court is not a stage for those with a sense of drama: the unpredictability of the judges and incomprehensibility of the procedure is dreadful. I cannot tell if it is going my way or not. Matrimonial judges try to ensure that both parties feel equally vindicated particularly if there are ongoing access issues.

The judge is there to make financial and access decisions based on factual representations and what is reasonable in light of the length and lifestyle of the marriage.

Access arrangements are formulaic; a midweek tea/overnight visit, every other weekend and half of the holidays, unless there are obvious areas of concern (abuse, etc).

Court is a stage for advocates and an arena of pain for the actual parties. Being in the same room as my sinister ex-husband (sometimes even trying to persuade the court clerks and my lawyers that I had not shown up, "Let's just go and settle this in a room together"), is horrifying.

The family court is charged with the atmosphere of people who once loved and now loathe each other. The stench of fear pervades, and the lighting strips all to the bone. Women's foundation cracks and lipstick 'bleeds' into their skin. People huddle in the corridors, by the lifts, on the stairs, whisperingly discussing their next move.

"The police were called twice," someone hissed, "and then the social services had to be called in."

Anxious grey faces speak in tremulous whispers.

The under belly of domestic bliss.

Only the lawyers speak the same language; divorcing spouses cannot understand a word the other says. Each thinks the other speaks in tongues – was there ever a shared syntax between them?

My team and I are looking for a room to confer in before our case is up. We pass rooms where faces, made ugly by tears, look up and in the background, the reasoning patter of legalese as their barristers try to prepare these wretches for the courtroom. The legal jargon reassures me. The comforts of this hell are a dead language and an archaic procedure.

We sit. My tea arrives (two tea bags – a surreal and disgusting moment when I fish the second sodden bag out of the polystyrene beaker) and so it begins: a boring recap of dates proposed and correspondence received, somewhat enlivened by the theatrical efforts of my barrister.

G's solicitor barges in, introduces herself all round, before punctuating her departure by slamming the door hard as she goes, leaving us all in stunned silence for a few moments.

"She has aged a good deal since last we met," my barrister laconically drawls.

Which is, I suppose, meant to be a reminder that he is firmly on my side.

"Whereas, of course, advocates are just prostitutes of the legal system – 'mouths for hire' are they not?" I refrain from adding.

Before the day is out my barrister has used the same anecdote about the judge twice. He is on automatic pilot, despite his fat fee.

Despite this, I never resented paying the barristers fees in the way I did the solicitors. Barristers have some *grasp* of the law, and it is a false economy to represent yourself unaided. Judges prefer professionals. Emotional civilians slow down proceedings. I came to learn that ambitious juniors are better value than the established advocates, clever and less self-satisfied, even willing (some of the time) to listen.

When G's lawyers make disgusting allegations about me, I bristle and mutter and my barrister turns back to me and hisses under his breath, "Stop f-ing and blinding."

I am struck dumb with shame.

The sound of dissent incenses the judges. Oh, and *never* cry in court.

* * *

My gynaecologist prescribes a host of pills to alleviate my excruciating monthly symptoms and later telephones to say, "Do not take them, it is all stress related. When the divorce is settled you will get better."

"Until then?" I ask.

"Stay home?" he suggests.

Good advice as one more stolen car (I keep leaving the keys in the ignition), will render me uninsurable.

I spend hours composing Francis a casual invitation,

"Sorry, too frantic." He replies.

"Do not worry." I offer as my soul shatters into shards of shame and humiliation.

* * *

Access used to be biased towards mummies and has now swung so far towards 'father's *rights*' that Colette's *needs* are forgotten.

Gargoyle does not want custody but damaging Colette might frighten me into agreeing a negligible settlement.

Puff should have alerted me to this, but G's tactics create legal fees and Puff's own child, who is the same age as Colette, is not in the firing line, at risk of being damaged.

If you have got young children, you are going to be dealing with their father long after the lawyers have gone. Getting as much money as you can may seem paramount, but the acrimony thereby created backfires on your children who have parents now hating each other even more.

Yep, and you are to blame as much as him, LW.

Puff is good at making me paranoid (and needy). He is encouraging me to believe that I am being followed and my phones are bugged. He even moots G's intent to present me as an alcoholic because Colette is five minutes late for collection!

* * *

Francis currently rings me regularly, which makes me feel a bit more supported and helps immensely.

* * *

I do not want to talk about our relative standards of living now as it is too banal. I should have got a van and taken what I wanted because possession is nine-tenths of the law. A man with a van whisking (at least) half the contents of our house away is not my style.

My neighbour says that if his access went wrong, "he" would, "abscond to Brazil."

Great!

* * *

Being in love with a married man is horrible.

Francis telephones, "Me and my family are going to Barbados next Wednesday. I'm not sure I had told you..."

I am speechless.

"Oh you are tired. Sorry to have disturbed you."

He signs off, doubtless relieved to have got that tricky chore off his chest.

I sit in the dark, tears rolling down my face. Eventually I text, "A breezy holiday plan brutally telling me all I need to know!"

All very dreary for him, I thought bitterly.

I walked into the night clinging to my phone but response came there none. Despair, how could he ignore my distress?

When I got home, I saw my phone was on silent!

There had been a flurry of messages and calls from him moments after I had sent my text.

My spirits soared.

I require so little. Where have I gone? I have been a secret for so long I have all but disappeared and seem to assume I deserve no more than to be treated like this at the beck and call and whim of other's needs.

Oh, for goodness sake.

"You seem to have read finality into my telling you that I will be away from the middle of next week. I cannot see my life changing, but I *do not* wish to exclude you."

Or more crudely, he'd like to have his cake and eat it, but... what can I say? He holds all the cards.

* * *

Sitting in the bank manager's office, "Is there anything else you want to discuss?" She asks me with bovine vacancy.

"I need a bank loan," I snap.

I tell her I am hoping for at least a couple of million out of my divorce settlement, whereupon she presses a key and £25,000 pops up in my account. I scoop my jaw off the floor and go... shopping!

I wanted a little memento of the cash before it drains into the lawyers' accounts.

The divorce has been going on for so long I have started toppling off pavements with exhaustion.

Terry tells me about his sister's break-up with a married man. "A foolish waste of seven years," he concludes.

"Foolish to embark upon it or to let it go on so long?" I ask with my heart in my mouth. Although his sister's circumstances *appear* similar to mine, they are not (I tell myself).

* * *

The pace is relentless and I keep ringing Puff – more costs – but I am terrified of doing something which can be used against me.

G does not understand that I am trying to remain civilised for Colette. No matter how disgustingly he behaves in court, I still smile and invite him in the next day.

* * *

Rubbish. I knew she hated him, and I found it completely discombobulating feeling disloyal about being pleased to see him, or her when he brought me home.

My friends think that trying to maintain a civil façade in front of Colette is weird, but our relationship was already "regulated hatred" as DW Harding once described Jane Austin's novels, before I left. Unhappy spouses are often masters of deceit.

* * *

The court orders a psychologist to interview me regarding the custody battle. He sits in my kitchen and *accuses* me of only having one O-level, which apparently proves I am an unfit mother. I kept mum because my numerous O-levels and A-levels, and first class degree, are irrelevant it seems to me as far as proving I am a fit mother or otherwise.

Another mistake.

Do not assume any of these 'professionals' (what is a court psychologist when it is at home anyway) have any sense at all. They are as impressed by the G's immense wealth, as everyone else, apparently. He is rich, therefore he must be an upstanding citizen, or anyway, we want to keep in with him in case... well you never know what the association might bring.

It is very weird.

Francis

"What would you advise me to do if I were your daughter and she asked you if she should indefinitely wait for her married lover?"

I ask and smile with bated breath as I skate forth where angels fear to tread.

Francis does not lie but he does not tell the truth either, because of course I am *not* his daughter.

* * *

The current access, where Colette moves from one parent to the other every other week, is catastrophic.

"*Please*, let me stay longer in each place, Daddy."

G turns away from her crumpled little face to roar at me,

"You *agreed* it!" He is actually trying to blame me for 'orders' I fought against tooth and nail.

Colette is ragged by the end of the holidays. The GP refuses to see her because G has threatened him. Not a single professional has ever stepped up for Colette when it counted. One woman at least wrote to Colette apologising for not being able to do more.

A gesture of inestimable value to Colette, who otherwise is in the eye of the storm alone and abandoned by all but me.

* * *

Francis is abroad and will not call.

* * *

I finished my finals today despite threatening texts from G even as I walk into the exam hall.

* * *

Later I collect Colette and find her playing in the sort of princess bedroom I always imagined for her. I cannot talk about that today. It makes the moles in my back bleed.

GP looks at bleeding moles and is adamant they must be dug out.

Thank God for insurance.

Dr Chopper, mole digger says, "40 is a difficult time for a woman." I had noticed that no one looks appreciatively at me any more but was happier not dwelling on it.

I wish I were dead but cannot be dead until Colette is safe.

The moles are benign, it transpires, unlike Dr Chopper.

Forty is a new experience: men do not stop and look any more, they stop and wait impatiently for you to cross without a backward glance. Hilarious that one should notice... and mind so.

* * *

Francis agrees to meet after a party,

"Unless you get stuck-in, in which case just call me." He offers discouragingly.

"Yes, yes. If I meet some divine man I will just call you and we'll do it another day. Does that sound good?"

Pause.

"No it does not sound good at all."

Well thank goodness for that.

Awful evening. Francis managed to make me feel like an obligation. I wish I was not so sure that he would breathe a huge sigh of relief if I went away.

I have given myself like a bunch of flowers to Francis, but he has no vase in which to arrange me.

I blurted out that I should have resisted calling him.

"Why didn't you?" he says.

Pretty devastating.

Before retiring, I cast a dispirited glance in my mobile's direction,

"I am afraid I was very tired. Had to work until 3am. Hope to see you soon – next week?" I mentally snuggle up to him again.

"Soon is lovely."

Poor Mama, she sounds so lonely. She should have pressed him to make a decision not let him treat her like a box of chocolates he could dip into when he felt like it. It is horrible.

* * *

Gargoyle chops Colette's soft curls off with kitchen scissors and posts them through the letterbox during the night.

* * *

I ask G if we can go to her birthday party together.

"It would add an hour to my journey, and I do not have time."

Colette asks if G can bring her home afterwards (still desperately trying to get Mummy and Daddy to do things without court orders).

"It depends on your mother!" G bellows, making me the Wicked Witch as usual.

"Of course, I will meet you there." I smile and get into my car. As soon as they are out of sight I light a cigarette with trembling hands.

Colette thinks G's got a girlfriend. The thought of his hands on anyone's flesh makes my skin crawl – for the woman's sake!

Sexual jealousy is obviously not going to be a problem for me, I conclude.

* * *

I ruminate on the idea of G and I taking Colette to a hotel for Christmas together. Making Colette split Christmas when her life is already so splintered is cruel, and she worries about Santa not finding her now.

The BBC is looking for divorced people who "come together at Christmas" to recount their experiences.

I telephone G and ask him, but he "does not want to say anything until he has spoken to his lawyers." So it has just become another controversy for the lawyers to wrangle over. Jesus.

I ask Puff if he is sitting comfortably before I tell him because lawyers do not like conciliatory gestures and his,

"Perhaps you had better not tell me then" is discouraging.

Puffle will let me know as soon as he hears anything from G's lawyers.

Colette returns from school shivering with excitement about Christmas, (she calls it "The Holidays").

Very PC.

* * *

Dread going home from Georgina's dinner in case the night postman (G) is lurking.

* * *

Francis telephones out of the blue and transports me out of the black, suggesting we might have supper if I am free?

Even if I were not free, I would free myself immediately.

* * *

Francis is away on the family holiday and it is shabby to call your mistress when you are with your wife.

Francis returns, and I bravely ask him what we are doing.

"We are making our way, slowly," he says.

My spirit soars.

Why does she let him treat her like a carpet?

Much later when he has brought me home and we have had 'tea' (climbed into bed), he says his headache has gone.

"All part of the service," I quip.

"I meant the pills, they are starting to work," he blusters, abashed.

"Indeed!" I say and we laugh.

And then he had to go.

* * *

The decree absolute will not be granted until a financial settlement is agreed. G seems determined to argue interminably.

* * *

I have stuck brown paper over my internal letterbox so that I do not see any nocturnal threats (or boarding school brochures, the latest answer to removing Colette from "her unfit mother's influence"), until morning.

If they want to get you, they get at your children.

As Marie Antoinette replied to the allegations of incest with her son, "It is very easy to twist the mind of a small child." What she saw done to him must have been like watching a Nazi using his surgical instrument on her boy's soft live brain.

I think she must have been very relieved when they chopped off her head.

* * *

G lies about his ability to cope with Colette and I no longer trust the judges to see through him and get the access right. Perhaps lots of fathers are actually hard done by, but the Gargoyle has brilliant access, which he does not always even take up. And yet he claims on paper to want more.

Male judges seem to assume that all mothers are maliciously determined to deny fathers access to their children.

I listened to a radio programme where the welfare officers (Cafcass) were saying that many of them had left the service because it was no longer concerned with children's *needs* but with parental *rights*.

My experience concurs with this.

* * *

G was hovering in my new café this morning. I did not recognise him at first and then realised that his stalking is out of control. My mouth is dry as I ignore him and sit down. We were in court yesterday with his solicitor reverting to G's original demand that Colette splits her week as "a sensible alternative to giving him sole custody"!

The judge did not go for it, but being up against a man with unlimited funds to litigate and who thinks treating children like suitcases is appropriate is terrifying. I never know what will happen in court and when things go my way it fuels his fury and provokes ever wilder behaviour.

He plonks himself down and growls at me, "Now, shall we make a plan for Friday?"

The latest court directions about the coming weekend have been unhelpfully ambiguous. There are so many confusing directions that we end up negotiating in cafés as well.

I regard the grotesque face mouthing at me before diving into my bag for cover. The Gargoyle is still chewing air when I re-emerge.

"I have not come here to have a conversation with you. I have come to have my coffee," I say, struggling not to panic, but my legs are jelly and my mouth so dry I can barely speak. He must not see how intimidated I am because he is a bully and they thrive on that.

His expression is inscrutable. The anger has made him irrational and impossible to read. He appears mad, really weird, and the sharp metallic taste of fear seeps into my mouth.

* * *

Conference day with barristers, QC, juniors and so on – 10 people in a plush room. "Am I paying for all this?" I ask on entering.

Haw haws all round. QC, "Hopefully your ex will get landed with all the costs."

Hopefully...

Puff has decided to pop an Akubra (worn by Australians in the outback) on top of his 4 feet five inch stature. But then I am in a fuschia and orange puffball dress so perhaps conferences have a funny effect generally.

Puff's assistant – why charge one set of fees when you can charge two – is wheeling a suitcase so I assume she is rushing off for the weekend afterwards, but the suitcase contains my case files.

So much paper... so many fees!

I coveted Puff's olive-skinned assistant's chic white coat. I watch enviously as she shrugs herself into it and heads off to her Gargoyle-free life at the end of the conference.

When it was all over, I bought myself a long white fur, an absurd purchase of symbolic importance, which I still wear with pride.

I do remember that coat. She looked liked the White Witch as she flew around the house in it making me laugh hysterically.

I have to remind myself not to be too entertained by these meetings because the advice affably dispensed is astronomically costly. I had learned early on that however comforting my lawyer was when I rang him over another incident, the fee clock was ticking softly in the background – sympathy is expensive when it comes to divorce lawyers.

The junior barrister asks what is left of the £25,000 bank loan.

"About £10,000?" I offer (I'm rubbish with money).

"I imagine there are some fees owing?" the QC drawls at Puff.

"Indeed," Puff concurs, "the latest costs will be submitted just prior to the court hearing."

I misheard "hearing" as "hanging".

The next legal bill will wipe me out and show the courts the hardship I endure because of my multimillionaire ex's *minimal* interim payments (I even qualify for milk benefits – hope some needy baby is not starving).

Temporary monthly payments (interim maintenance) are significant as they ultimately define your needs. If you are seen to be managing on a pittance, that is what you will get.

No one cares how these *tactics* will affect my child's *actual* Christmas.

Why would anyone *choose* to make their living from the misery of others? Many of the matrimonial celebrities are Catholics, so perhaps it is vicarious living (you never hear of them encouraging their client to return to the matrimonial fold and thereby stop racking up fees at the same time as sticking to their vows).

Most of the meeting concerned how ongoing legal fees were to be funded.

"High priority stuff," I quipped and Puff guffawed, "Touché Cecily." (To my increasing irritation as his fees grew like beanstalks, he had insisted on this faux intimacy from the outset.)

He chuckled and reverted to fees owing, racking up more fees in the process!

They forget they are discussing your *life*.

Puff makes it clear that if I cannot pay soon, representation will be withdrawn. So we aren't 'mates', as he constantly claims, after all. Your lawyer is not your friend. Puff would be representing G if he had asked first.

Think of yourself as the rent if it keeps you off the phone and costs down. Do not fight for a settlement only to hand it all over to lawyers.

* * *

A QC once gave me a tip, "Take £500 in £50 notes and toss them out of the window while you are chatting to your lawyer. When the hour is up, and the money has gone... You will soon learn to chat less next time."

They conclude I should accept G's offer of our tiny London house, to borrow money against to pay my legal fees.

"£100,000 might be enough to be going on with," Puff drawls.

"You'll be downgrading to a flat soon anyway," someone tosses out.

I am aghast. I have been led to believe there will be less disparity in our lifestyles, not more, post-divorce.

Nothing any of them say diminishes my incredulity that thousands of pounds of legal fees later, I now stand to lose my home.

Puff's cello playing partner crashes into the room waving papers from G's solicitors offering... not much, according to Ms Du Pre, who says he is playing games and is clearly determined to have his day in court.

"Just as you always said," Puff defers to me, so I am now more on top of things than my expensive legal team.

Super!

* * *

Shortly afterwards I receive the news that The Bank of Scotland had refused the loan I needed to pay my legal fees. Puff says if his fees aren't paid next week, he will no longer represent me.

"What will I do?" I cried plaintively to this lawyer who said we were 'mates'.

"I do not know, Cecily," Puff offered, indifferently.

"You might apply for legal aid... but I do not think you would get it. And my firm does not do legal aid cases."

The only plus to this financial panic is that it has distracted me from the electrifying prospect of seeing Francis again (last time I was physically sick with anticipation, and worrying about my breath, despite frantic teeth brushing all evening).

Oh Mum, what a muddle.

CHAPTER EIGHTEEN

"Certain women should be struck regularly, like gongs."

Noel Coward, *Private Lives Act 3*

I go to Colette's school concert. The Gargoyle is already there, looming large and somehow preventing me from hugging Colette.

She finds me at the end and says plaintively, "Why can't I go to Daddy for tea?"

I concur with twisted insides and Gargoyle sweeps Colette up onto his shoulders and walks around the melee of parents with tears streaming down his face!

Quite a display.

As soon as we are outside, G's tears dry up as he grabs Colette's hand and marches off with her at a great pace. "Bye, bye, Mummy. See you later." She turns and anxiously waves.

I run after them and suggest we share a taxi. G bellowed back, "I cannot possibly afford a taxi!"

Whereupon Colette joins in, "Yes Mummy, Daddy cannot possibly afford taxis. You should learn to walk." And sticks her tongue out at me as they disappear.

I should have told the Gargoyle to sod off, as I am within my rights to do. But you do not engage in public scenes for your child's sake. If I had said "no" I would look unreasonable because no one knows that I will spend agonising hours not knowing when Colette will come home, suffering the agony of longing to hold her again.

Waiting for her to return to her routine of supper time, bath time, story time and bedtime kisses. When will they come?

No one would believe a parent could be so cruel, so I acquiesce to G's ad hoc access demands. The whole point of 'access' is to establish routine and avoid disruptive negotiations on the hoof.

We had court orders and hoofs galore, and unbound disruption.

I remind myself that Colette will come home later, and I will kiss her. Much later. Predictably.

My heart beats like a wounded bird. The uncertainty every school event now presents. Machinations such as G's are not unique but noteworthy nevertheless, and my mind becomes increasingly fragile as I try to manage it all.

Doc's given me Prozac.

"So that's all right then."

CHAPTER NINETEEN

"'Tis hard if all is false that I advance
A fool must now and then be right, by chance."
William Cowper, *Conversation*

High Court

Application to increase the interim maintenance order.

I have no money for Christmas presents let alone fees, so it seems absurd to spend thousands in court to get a bit extra every month. I am advised it is a 'necessary tactic'.

I dread these court days now, mostly because the prospect of being anywhere near the Gargoyle makes me ill.

I was dismayed when Puff commented on the way to our first *financial* hearing, "This is where it gets interesting."

So all Puff's 'concern' over Colette's access arrangements was a bluff. Good financial settlements are what make reputations. The sad business of apportioning a child's time is galling, even for lawyers.

G presents a document to the court arguing that Colette and I should live on benefits in a council house, and I should be a cleaner.

G's QC looked a bit bashful. I am already receiving milk vouchers and tax credits (which I will have to repay when a settlement is agreed). The lawyers say it is demeaning for me to receive benefits, but I assure them the money is currently vital.

I wear white and no makeup for court (I want to feel clean).

We have to argue for G to be told to give full disclosure about his finances, which you would have thought was par for the course, but everything is arguable and I have enough experience of insane judgments to be leery.

Yer never know.

We lost.

The judge decided that G can afford more but that I can *manage* until the final hearing, which is imminent according to the judge.

In fact, inevitably, it was *years* before a final settlement was reached.

District judges usually get it wrong in my experience.

Perhaps I was unlucky...

Perhaps.

My 'team' reconvened in Starbucks for a post-court debrief.

Puff, itching to get away after my defeat, told me I now have to be *seen* by the courts to go into debt. It was like being advised by a knight in shining armour to find an alternative bloke.

I was brought up to regard debt as A Bad Thing.

Precedents are crucial. Anything before the (access or financial) settlement sets a precedent, which must later be argued against if you want a change.

I consider appointing new lawyers, to advise me on my current lawyers, whose advice I no longer trust.

CHAPTER TWENTY

"They went, the Ghost and Scrooge, across the hall, to a door at the back of the house. It opened before them, and disclosed a long, bare, and melancholy room, made barer still by lines of plain deal forms and desks. At one end of these a lonely boy was reading near a feeble fire; and Scrooge sat down upon a form, and wept to see his poor forgotten self as he used to be."

Charles Dickens, Scrooge

The First Christmas.

Oh, God here we go.

There are both custody and full disclosure financial hearings before Christmas.

We have agreed that I will stay near Lurch at Christmas and G will bring Colette over when he feels like it.

For years afterwards Colette used to ring me asking, "Are you at your hotel, Mama?"

So my imagined proximity *was* reassuring.

* * *

Francis will go home to his family for Christmas.

***

Today, we are all interviewed by Cafcass officers (part of G's ploy for custody). Their offices are unutterably depressing. What the hell are we doing here? These services are for the dispossessed, not the rich. I sit on a child-size plastic chair and wait opposite a desperate looking Indian family whose translator is on her way. But they do not understand this and become increasingly agitated, perhaps their misery is not so very different from mine.

Two teenagers bear down on me with patronising smiles. They ask me questions, and I do not know where to begin. How can I describe what is happening without sounding barking mad? My gravest error was to be reasonable and calm as though I have nothing to fear. There are no school or doctors' reports validating any of G's complaints, so they will see him for what he is, an angry man.

I have a fatal tendency to overestimate professionals.

James is furious with me, "He will be saying all sorts of horrific things about you. Take off your gloves and fight back!"

"Well I have done it now."

But he was right. The court psychologists and Cafcass officers take what people say as read.

I ring and ask them. "We have to believe what each person says," they say.

Why? Everybody lies, why would litigating spouses be any different?

* * *

I dine with Freddy. I thought I would be glad of the distraction after a horrible day in court. He is awfully dreary these days.

And so fat!

He makes overtures to me all evening. How desperate do I look? Some of my friends do the oddest things since I reverted to singledom.

Freddy pinched my bottom as he left (thinking it would seal the deal?).

* * *

The Christmas "Holiday" finally arrives and the lawyers close their offices and go home as G collects Colette, early of course, banging on the door and shouting as we rush to complete her packing. And I am left alone. Completely alone.

Eva our nanny crept in to hug me before she went off to Poland for Christmas. Thank God, as I had taken a heavy dose of Valium and would have missed my train to Lurchland otherwise.

I take a train and move through the journey as if in a dream. Unearthly, ghastly things fill my mind.

People sense I am in extremis and are surreally kind: the taxi man left his taxi (unheard of these days) to get a trolley for me, and the train guard comes back to help me off the train as she promised she would.

Gargoyle brings Colette to my hotel room and immediately rushes downstairs to close his account so we cannot have tea on his bill. He is oblivious to Colette's distress at the lack of civility between her parents.

Each time I see Colette, she looks more exhausted and filthy and we have bath time as she wants. But there are no ducks and letters to stick around the bath, and my heart swells up into my throat so that my chest is tight and I hold my breath to keep my sadness bottled inside.

You cling to small things.

Colette clings to me.

* * *

Colette says she could not find her stocking because it was not by her bed. I ask G where Colette was sleeping.

"She sleeps everywhere," he says and continues bellowing at the waitress who has brought a whole bottle of champagne instead of one glass each.

Colette hardly looks at me when she is with Gargoyle now. She feels guilty wherever she looks, so she looks away. G goes off somewhere and she puts her head in my lap repeating, "I'm a baby. I'm a baby."

No more.

After a heartbreaking lunch, we go for a howling walk. G grabs Colette's hand and dashes across the hotel gardens, and I am alone in the bitter wind.

CHAPTER TWENTY

I close my eyes and want to die.

* * *

I am desperate to go home but trains do not run on Boxing Day, so I ring Anna Skips who has a house guest delighted to give me a lift.

A reprieve.

And that was it, our first Christmas.

The access order arrives – custody denied.

I have no sense of triumph. Too battered.

* * *

No word from Francis.

Where is he?

CHAPTER TWENTY-ONE

"It's nice to meet serious people

And hear them explain their views:

Your concern for the rights of women

Is especially welcome news.

I'm sure you'd never exploit one;

I expect you'd rather be dead;

I'm thoroughly convinced of it –

Now can we go to bed?"

Wendy Cope, From June to December, A Serious Person

A New Year?

I receive an exorbitant bill from Puff for 'child issues' today. I call him on it as access has been set. He refers to a recent conversation when he asked me how Colette was.

"Next time you ask me and I (politely) reply, it is incumbent upon you to point out that you will be billing me for my good manners!"

I write a formal letter stating that he cannot do anything further regarding Colette without written instructions from me.

They are sharks!

* * *

Email from another mummy telling me her divorce is absolute. I battle with envy, lose the fight, and admit I am green! Everyone seems to get a better, swifter deal than me.

An earlier QC expostulated upon seeing me walking through the Temple last week, "You cannot still be at it!"

Even by the dreary standards of the courts, my divorce is seemingly interminable.

* * *

I bumped into some Lurch neighbours today. No one says hello, so I do not have to say hello back.

Sweet.

* * *

Days later, I am sitting with Francis in a bar with flutes of champagne and I am trying to control my breathing, I have a 'drunk and shrunk' feeling like Alice in Wonderland. I seem to be getting smaller as my surroundings grow larger.

Francis leans in, "Tell me what it is, and you will feel better."

He says this kind of thing to reassure himself that he is sticking around to help me, with no ulterior motive of his own, and if he keeps our relationship within the realms of help and comfort all will be well.

CHAPTER TWENTY-ONE

I mumble something about not being able to bear it any more and Francis assumes I'm talking about my divorce. His patter about how it will eventually be resolved *et cetera* makes me want to screech,

"It is nothing to do with that that, it is us! I love you and if you are just being kind, then I want to curl up and die."

Obviously I do not say any of this, I just smile enigmatically and what his regard signifies is a mystery.

The only clue comes when he interrupts my prattling and describes us as being "like children at the round pond in the gardens of Les Tuileries in Paris... launching boats with gay abandon."

Just a crumb but sweet enough to put me back in my bubble until he says, "I must be off, or I will be late for my little (21-year-old) girl."

My heart contracts and the bubble bursts.

* * *

Please, please do not leave me.

CHAPTER TWENTY-TWO

"Truth, when witty, is the wittiest of all things."
Julius and Augustus Hare, Guesses at Truth

The Mistress

I have supper with a gossipy friend who takes my breath away when he says, "I bumped into a pissed Nigella last night, she tells me you are in love with Francis Blank. You must be longing to tell someone. Lovely to be able to chatter away knowing you are safe. Do you think his wife has cottoned on yet? She is rather a good sort, actually."

I gaze at him. Speechless.

"Of course he has had these little affairs from time to time, they have been married forever with endless children and so on, but you must keep in mind there is no possibility whatsoever that he would ever leave her. Away games are frowned upon but endured. Do not be fooled, she always knows what he is up to... count on that!"

He settled himself back in his chair to assess the inroads his assertions have carved across my heart.

"I simply had to tell you, you are such a dear old thing. You cannot possibly be ready to launch into the next Big Thing? Rebound relationships are always a disaster, always."

I fled home and called Francis.

"Hello." Came his soft voice and my tears flowed.

I would tell him everything, and he would gently explain that it would be all right. Difficult, but all right in the end.

And he did.

* * *

The following day there was a piece in the paper about Francis Blank being seen around town with a mystery girl.

Francis sent me a message telling me that he must repair the devastation this had brought on his family. I should, "try to get on with my life."

I telephoned Nigella, "You'll hear from him. Do not worry, he just needs time to plaster things up."

A newspaper must be the worst way to discover your marriage is over, but I had no way of knowing how determined he was in those days.

* * *

The high court hearing for the final settlement has taken so long that it is deemed necessary by the courts to send Colette to boarding school. I fought it tooth and nail but

Colette says it was a good thing she went. An end to those harrowing access handovers at last!

* * *

My lawyer tells me to dress down for the high court proceedings (he obviously remembers the fluffy chiffon number I wore in chambers).

* * *

I go to Starbucks with Elizabeth in the morning of the high court proceedings.

"You really need to go," she says.

I do not want her to go. I want to stay in Starbucks.

I climb into my battered car and make my way to... hell.

High Court

A surreal moment when my QC stands and says, "I call my first witness" (as they do), and I gaze around the room and suddenly realise that they are waiting for me.

You can choose to sit or stand while giving evidence. I sit – my knees are jelly. I am told to direct all my answers to the judge, which is awkward, as it seems so rude to turn away from the barrister questioning you.

Giving evidence is easy – you just have to tell the truth.

Once I had got though all the "swearing by almighty God" stuff, the rest was a breeze. After a couple of questions from the judge, I rose to my feet with growing confidence, batting answers back with sanguinity (although my heart would have been beating like a drum had it not been for the beta blockers prescribed by my GP – a useful tip).

At the end of a divorce hearing everyone must feel they have had their say (G had a *lot* to say), because in matrimonial cases judges aim to reduce the acrimony, and letting people vent their spleen helps achieve this, sometimes.

Humour

Gargoyle, desperately trying to make a point about my extravagance, explains to Her Ladyship what Prada is.

"Mr G, you may take it as read that I know *all* the shops in London," she snaps.

Judges often tell you to take a break and see if you can cobble together a deal in the corridor – fat chance of that with G.

My QC says, "It is a simple case Cecily, and you will be all right."

QCs are a bit like doctors – unruffled by the individual circumstances. They are brought in on a case and they get on with it – and I do not actually think they do engage much with the individual's circumstances. Or perhaps I was just unlucky...

Elizabeth had advised me to make a list of chattels that I wanted from the house. This is good advice because if you do not ask you will not get. And I got more than I expected because it was now in the judge's gift not G's.

I could not see the point because I knew he would say "no" to everything. But as it transpired, my little list provided a moment of merriment, which did a good deal to dilute the dreariness of the high court proceedings, introducing as it did "The Case of the Golden Bananas: A Tale of Matrimonial Madness."

I had taken the gilt bananas on departure because they were so truly hideous, and G adored them. There! I admit it! It was a deliberately provocative act. I never for one moment imagined that I would actually have to live with the things for as long as I did, but I knew that their departure would send G into an almighty spin. Gargoyle made an impassioned speech about the empty space on the dining table where the golden bananas had once shone forth so brightly.

Her Ladyship listened earnestly and then wryly suggested that we might share the bananas between us? "One each, Mr G?"

"No, no that will not do at all!" came G's voice booming back from the other side of the court (which was a relief as I certainly did not want to get stuck with them).

I struggled to contain my giggles as she gravely pronounced on the matter, I was to get money in lieu of a lovely bunch of bananas. Hurrah!

The Settlement

Her Ladyship said she would hand judgment down next week. They do this to enable you to distance yourself from the awfulness of the process. When you have been locked in litigation, the judgment feels like the only thing in the world that matters.

It is not.

G is clearly advised by his lawyers, who had been sitting at the back of the courtroom, that he was likely to be ordered to pay far more than I had offered to take. So before judgment could be handed down they hurriedly settled, for rather more than I had previously asked for. However, needless to say, G refused to pay my costs saying that the matter should be decided by the court.

We returned to court and told the judge of the settlement. She looked at my QC over her glasses and said quietly, "I see. So I no longer need to say what I would have ordered". My QC blushes furiously, realising that he has settled for less than the judge would have ordered. Just my luck.

"What about costs?" I hiss. He whispers back that this is not the time. By now I felt courage from my fury and the judge's obvious sympathy, I whispered back. "Ask for them NOW". He did.

G was ordered to pay my legal costs and totally lost his temper, roaring at the judge about the unfairness of the court process towards the litigant who argues in person. The judge had anticipated this (they have seen it all before) and reminded him how many allowances she had made him for precisely this reason.

She knew perfectly well that he had chosen to represent himself (a common intimidation tactic), but noted that he had had legal representation up to the hearing itself and had been intending to re-employ his QC to argue costs tomorrow. She was not having any nonsense about unfairness in her court. Costs were decided there and then. A small victory, but not worth the horrors that had preceded it.

That shut him up.

I leave High Court for the last time on a Friday afternoon.

* * *

Tim sweetly comes for drinks explaining, "Once you have been thorough it yourself there is an almost morbid interest in hearing about someone else's."

I do not agree. I cannot bear being regaled with divorce stories, but I have written mine down in the hope it might provide a rough guide to untying the knot as decently as you can for your children's sakes. They deserve the best you can manage.

Make them weapons at your peril.

* * *

Days later and I am still carrying the vestiges of fear that someone will ring to tell me that the final judgment has been overturned and we are going back to court. I tell Douglas it feels as though I have been wearing a peculiar pair of spectacles, which were distorting my vision, and now the stress is alleviated, the specs are off, but it is taking me an unexpectedly long time to adjust to my new perspective.

And Colette's absence.

I find it very difficult to believe I need no longer be fearful. I hang on to the response that I got from Puff when I asked him if my lot were going to be bossy about what I wear to court the next week (when everyone trailed back for final costs).

"You can be as glam as you like, Cecily."

Which more than anything, makes me feel that it is done.

Postscript

I told my lawyer during a court lunch one day about me choosing Kate in *The Taming of the Shrew* for my marriage reading. He was agog, "What is your understanding of the scene where she says she will lay herself underfoot?" he asked.

I answered easily, "When you love true, you trust, and so can submit fully, safe in the knowledge that your submission will not be abused."

"That implies a huge degree of trust, Cecily," he countered, devilish little rocket scientist that he is.

"Yes, Puff. I did not take my wedding vows lightly. If I had not trusted him, I should not have married him. It seems I was wrong."

CHAPTER TWENTY-TWO

I hope I have not completely lost the ability to trust to such a degree. I also hope that it will not always be a mistake to do so. Douglas was furious about my choice of verse as were many others at the time, "How could you?" and so on but they all take the 20th century reading and regard it as a completely anti-women's lib text thereby completely missing Shakespeare's point. That real love can submit because there is no risk of abuse, total submission implies complete faith, which you need for a really happy union I think. G probably thought (as did all my friends it would seem), that I was prostrating myself as a willing doormat. As it happens I was in fact inviting him to raise his game.

I may have been a blind fool, but I still think he was the greater loser.

* * *

The battle is over and I feel oddly deflated. I have got a bit of financial security but Colette has gone... and Francis? I still do not know.

End of Book One

I close the last of the leather-bound volumes and sit back. So many questions answered and so many new ones to ponder. Whatever happened next? Will I find another box of volumes somewhere in the house?

I walk slowly away down the street. I do not have the strength or courage to go beyond this now. I just need LW to come back and explain. I need my Mummy to come home.

Fin

ABOUT THE AUTHOR

Isolde has recently finished drafting a potential prequel to *The Diary of a Divorce* called, *A Model Life*, about a ferociously shy girl who is plucked from obscurity and into the international fashion scene. Extraordinary success in virtual isolation from friends and family leaves her vulnerable to the pitfalls of the industry, which she must overcome to survive.

The young girl is of course the woman who becomes Cecily in *The Diary of a Divorce*.

Isolde has contributed to *The Spectator Magazine* (Frank Johnson), *The Sunday Telegraph* (Charles Moore), *Boulevard Magazine* (an English speaking publication in Paris), and is an occasional playwright. She has appeared in numerous television and radio slots in the US and UK.

Isolde recently submitted a short story to *Woman's Hour*, based on her play *Medea's Daughter* about child abuse, which they are considering adapting for radio.

Isolde lives in England and is widely referred to as 'The Poster Girl for Moving On' among her colleagues and friends.

Never Give Up!